Stressed Out in School?

Learning to Deal With
Academic Pressure

Titles in the Issues in Focus Today *series:*

Am I Fat?
The Obesity Issue for Teens
ISBN-13: 978-0-7660-2527-1
ISBN-10:   0-7660-2527-6

Beyond Bruises
The Truth About Teens and Abuse
ISBN-13: 978-0-7660-3064-0
ISBN-10:   0-7660-3064-4

Bioethics
Who Lives, Who Dies, and Who Decides?
ISBN-13: 978-0-7660-2546-2
ISBN-10:   0-7660-2546-2

Child Labor Today
A Human Rights Issue
ISBN-13: 978-0-7660-2682-7
ISBN-10:   0-7660-2682-5

China in the 21st Century
A New World Power
ISBN-13: 978-0-7660-2684-1
ISBN-10:   0-7660-2684-1

The Evolution Debate
Darwinism vs. Intelligent Design
ISBN-13: 978-0-7660-2911-8
ISBN-10:   0-7660-2911-5

Fighting the AIDS and HIV Epidemic
A Global Battle
ISBN-13: 978-0-7660-2683-4
ISBN-10:   0-7660-2683-3

Islam
Understanding the History, Beliefs, and Culture
ISBN-13: 978-0-7660-2686-5
ISBN-10:   0-7660-2686-8

Peanut Butter, Milk, and Other Deadly Threats
What You Should Know About Food Allergies
ISBN-13: 978-0-7660-2529-5
ISBN-10:   0-7660-2529-2

A Pro/Con Look at Homeland Security
Safety vs. Liberty After 9/11
ISBN-13: 978-0-7660-2914-9
ISBN-10:   0-7660-2914-X

The Scoop on What to Eat
What You Should Know About Diet and Nutrition
ISBN-13: 978-0-7660-3066-4
ISBN-10:   0-7660-3066-0

Superfood or Superthreat
The Issue of Genetically Engineered Food
ISBN-13: 978-0-7660-2681-0
ISBN-10:   0-7660-2681-7

Weapons of Mass Destruction
The Threat of Chemical, Biological, and Nuclear Weapons
ISBN-13: 978-0-7660-2685-8
ISBN-10:   0-7660-2685-X

Welcome to America?
A Pro/Con Debate Over Immigration
ISBN-13: 978-0-7660-2912-5
ISBN-10:   0-7660-2912-3

Stressed Out in School?

Learning to Deal With
Academic Pressure

ISSUES IN FOCUS TODAY

Stephanie Sammartino McPherson

 Enslow Publishers, Inc.
40 Industrial Road
Box 398
Berkeley Heights, NJ 07922
USA

http://www.enslow.com

For my mother, Marion, a dedicated and enthusiastic teacher for many years; for my father, Angelo, a retired Marine Corps officer and teacher who brought his love of history to the classroom; and in memory of my mother-in-law, Marie McPherson, who made learning joyful for a generation of students.

Library of Congress Cataloging-in-Publication Data

McPherson, Stephanie Sammartino.
    Stressed out in school? : learning to deal with academic pressure / Stephanie Sammartino McPherson.
        p. cm. — (Issues in focus today)
    Includes bibliographical references and index.
    Summary: "Examines the stress and academic pressure students of all ages encounter, including early education, homework, standardized tests, college applications, peer pressure, and alternative learning styles"—Provided by publisher.
    ISBN-13: 978-0-7660-3069-5
    ISBN-10: 0-7660-3069-5
    1. Students—Mental health—United States—Juvenile literature. 2. Stress management—United States—Juvenile literature. 3. Stress (Psychology)—Prevention—Juvenile literature. 4. Students—Academic workload—United States—Psychological aspects. I. Title.
    LB3430.M38 2010
    371.7'13—dc22

                                    2008040339

Printed in the United States of America
052010 Lake Book Manufacturing, Inc., Melrose Park, IL
10 9 8 7 6 5 4 3 2

To Our Readers: We have done our best to make sure all Internet Addresses in this book were active and appropriate when we went to press. However, the author and the publisher have no control over and assume no liability for the material available on those Internet sites or on other Web sites they may link to. Any comments or suggestions can be sent by e-mail to comments@enslow.com or to the address on the back cover.

♻ Enslow Publishers, Inc., is committed to printing our books on recycled paper. The paper in every book contains 10% to 30% post-consumer waste (PCW). The cover board on the outside of each book contains 100% PCW. Our goal is to do our part to help young people and the environment too!

Illustration Credits: BananaStock, pp. 5, 89; Digital Vision, pp. 5, 21, 23, 57, 81, 99, 103; EyeWire Images, pp. 30, 45, 92; Getty Images, pp. 5, 7, 13, 19, 97; iStockphoto, pp. 53, 78; Library of Congress, p. 85; Photos.com, pp. 5, 32, 63; Courtesy of Marion Sammartino, p. 16; Shutterstock, pp. 5, 10, 27, 35, 38, 41, 48, 61, 69, 71, 73, 95, 101.

Cover Illustration: iStockphoto (large photo); BananaStock (small inset photo).

Contents

Acknowledgments

I would like to thank all the parents, teachers, counselors, and students who agreed to speak with her, including Claudia Porter, Jane Chapin, Joanne Ward, Kimberly Sanford, Cynthia Ford, Dorene Jorgensen, Joanna Hersch, Jeffrey Doyle, Dalene Landes, Bryan Carr, Sarah Mansfield, Autumn Nabors, Jennifer Coleman, Paul Fleisher, Mickey VanDerwerker, Gayle Hamilton, Marshall W. Trammell, Jr., Angelo Sammartino, Marion Sammartino, Julia Johnson, Colleen Twomey, and Maryanne Kiley. As always, thanks to my husband, Richard, for his unwavering help and encouragement.

Kids on the Fast Track

1

In the late 1800s, a class of young women at Vassar College braved freezing winter weather for an extraordinary event. Huddled in darkness on the rooftop of the college observatory, they shrieked with excitement. Thousands of shooting stars were crossing the sky. A meteor shower did not happen every night. The students were glad that their teacher, Maria Mitchell, had wakened them for the splendid sight. Her enthusiasm made astronomy fascinating to them too.

The first woman astronomer in the United States, Maria Mitchell loved everything about teaching—except giving grades. She liked to joke that if a student came to class well prepared, that student deserved an A for achievement. If a student came to class partially prepared, that student deserved an A for effort. And if a student came to class totally unprepared, that student deserved an A for courage in daring to appear at all.[1] Rarely did the last situation occur.

Maria Mitchell expected hard work from her students, and she got it. Almost all educators will tell you that this is the way it should be—students working hard for the love of learning. But it does not always turn out this way. Instead of an adventure, school has become a source of stress to some students. They worry about their classroom performance and their class ranking. They fear that if they fall behind, they will not get into a good college. For such students, the subject matter becomes secondary to the grades they earn. The pressure they feel may actually make it harder for them to learn.

Of course, not all pressure is harmful. In fact, it is almost impossible to imagine a world without it. Adults face pressure to earn enough money, pressure to do their jobs well, and pressure to please family and friends. They have deadlines and responsibilities to meet. These demands can be good things as long as they do not become overwhelming.

The same thing is true of academic pressure. It is not all bad. For example, a Spanish test on Friday may be just the spur a student needs to learn those new vocabulary words. In a similar way, writing a history paper can give someone a chance to explore people and ideas in greater depth than in the classroom. Ideally, this should be something the student enjoys doing.

The question is not how to free students from all pressure. It is how much pressure and what kind of assignments make for the best learning situations. What works well for one student may not necessarily work well for another. Yet teachers lack the time and resources to individualize assignments for every student. Like many of the children in their classrooms, they often feel anxious and overworked. Some educators and parents believe that much of the problem has to do with the growing demands placed on teachers by school districts and the government. Children are being asked to master material at younger ages. In many instances, teachers are judged not so much on the quality of their instruction as on how well their students perform on standardized tests. This can be frustrating for everyone concerned.

The Youngest Students

Even kindergarten is not what it used to be. Several generations ago, children learned to read in first grade. Now reading instruction usually begins in kindergarten. In certain schools, students are tested repeatedly to make sure they are mastering skills quickly enough. Some kids do fine at the accelerated pace. They learn to read easily and move on to harder books. But others struggle. One school district in Buffalo, New York, made six hundred first graders attend summer school to boost their

> **The question is not how to free schools from all pressure. It is how much pressure and what kind of assignments make for the best learning situations.**

reading proficiency. Forty-two percent of those children in the summer school had to repeat the first grade.[2] Holly Hultgren of Lafayette Elementary School in Boulder, Colorado believes that pressure can cause some students to lose interest in schoolwork as early as third grade. This is called "burnout."[3] Children who excelled in first and second grades may begin to find school boring. They want more time to play and relax.

Pressure in Middle School

What is true in first grade is true throughout all twelve grades. For example, in Chesterfield County, Virginia, school officials have condensed a three-year math program into two years. That way students are ready for algebra in eighth grade instead of ninth. Many teachers feel this is important because at the end

School pressure can begin at the earliest levels. Kindergarten is much more academic than it used to be, with reading and writing instruction and, often, an emphasis on testing.

of the school year, all students in Virginia must take a series of state-mandated tests called the SOLs, or Standards of Learning. Some sixth and seventh graders were having a hard time passing the SOL in math. If enough students at a school do poorly on the test, that school could lose its state accreditation. The school would no longer receive state funding. Parents might decide to send their children somewhere else. The school board vice chair, Marshall W. Trammell, Jr., thinks the more intense math curriculum is a good idea. He cites studies indicating that students need to take advanced math courses in high school in order to meet the challenges of the twenty-first century. But he also has concerns. "Regardless of the research, I'm still not convinced that all kids are ready for algebra in eighth grade," he says "But a lot of students may be."[4]

College in High School?

The "fast track" continues in high school, where students face tougher challenges than their parents did. In some schools, eligible students are encouraged to take honors and Advanced Placement (AP) classes. These are college level courses, but they are taught in high school. Students who do well in such classes get an added boost to their grade point average. For example, an A in a regular class equals four points. But an A in an AP class earns five points. To receive college credit, students must take an AP test at the end of the year. They must cram in studying for this test with all their other school requirements. Often they find themselves getting insufficient sleep. This makes them less able to keep up with the demands of jam-packed schedules. According to a survey done in 2004, more than fifty percent of U.S. teenagers admit to being "stressed out all of the time or sometimes." Two thirds of the students polled cited academics as the chief cause of their stress.[5]

Child psychologist David Elkind captured the essence of the problem in the title of his groundbreaking book *The Hurried*

Child: Growing Up Too Fast Too Soon. Elkind is concerned about the practice of teaching subject matter in earlier and earlier grades. He calls this an "assembly line" approach to education.[6] "There is a tendency to speed up the assembly line," he writes, "to increase production. Why not put in as much at kindergarten as at first grade? Why not teach fourth grade math at grade two? Indeed, as one professor mused, why not teach philosophy at grade three?"[7] Some observers might call Elkind's words a good description of the current educational scene. However, his book was published in 1981. Clearly the phenomenon of urging children to achieve more at younger ages has been around for a while.

Psychologist William Crain, who agrees with Elkind, sums up the prevalent attitude in his book *Reclaiming Childhood*: "When it comes to children's learning, we assume that faster is better."[8] But, as Crain points out, there are many fallacies in this view. By pushing children academically, schools may be forcing them to neglect other important aspects of their development. These include creative ability and a deepening appreciation of nature. Crain agrees with noted psychologist Jean Piaget that intellectual growth cannot be rushed. Each child has his or her own inner schedule.[9] Some are ready to read early; others later. The slower developing child is not less capable than his more rapidly developing classmates. His natural abilities are simply unfolding at a slower rate. This is not a problem unless schools make it a problem.

Why are children being pushed so quickly? Does this pressure better prepare them to meet the demands of adult life? Does it help them get better jobs? Does it make them happier? These are some of the questions that parents, educators, and students face every day.

School Daze?

Marion Sammartino, a retired teacher and the mother of this book's author, used to write an educational column called *School Days*. Weekly she dispensed advice for parents on how to motivate their children and prepare them to be good students. One morning, when the newspaper arrived, Sammartino was startled to see a misprint in her column. Instead of *School Days*, the headline read *School Daze*! At first the mistake annoyed her. Then she had to laugh. "School Daze" sounded like an appropriate description of the fast-paced schedule and accompanying stress many students faced both during and after school. Simply put, these students had too much to do and too little time to do it. Sammartino decided that her next column would deal with the issue.

As the first chapter showed, even very young children can become dazed by the demands of school. Play and socialization have taken a back seat to academics. One mother in Virginia described her son's kindergarten homework as "overwhelming." Writing ten words that rhyme, making a puppet from a paper bag, or writing a story about a raindrop sounds simple to older children, but it can be anxiety-provoking for five-year-olds. Although Jason (not his real name) was often sick with sore throats, his illnesses did not excuse him from making up assignments. "Sometimes [Jason] threw himself on the floor, screamed, and cried, 'I hate homework,'" his mother said.[1]

In the course of the year, Jason and his classmates were strongly encouraged to do a science project. Jason chose a project about the stalactites and stalagmites that grow from the tops and bottoms of caves. With the help of his parents, he grew crystals from table salt and Epsom salt to replicate these formations. Jason's project had to include an objective, hypothesis, procedures, and results. His mother typed up the report and put it on a presentation board.

> **Even very young children can become dazed by the demands of school. Play and socialization have taken a back seat to academics.**

At one time such a project might have been considered more suitable for children in third or fourth grade. Jason's mother is concerned about the pressure being placed on her son. "[Jason] is focused on being a boy, on playing and having fun," she said. "[Children] should be allowed to do that."[2]

The principal of a prestigious private school in New York voiced much the same sentiment when reviewing a child's application for kindergarten. "I think the biggest gift you can give kids today—when programs are pressured and kindergartens look like first grades did before—is time," explained the principal.

In deferring the application, he believed he was acting in the child's best interests. "Rushing this child with a set of expectations that seem to not match his normal development seems to be a mistake."[3]

The push to master reading, as measured by tests, may even contribute to so-called fourth-grade slump. First observed in the 1960s, the slump refers to a slow-down from the more rapid progress children made in earlier grades. "We kill them with tests in 3rd grade," Virginia teacher Gina Defalco told reporters from *Newsweek*. "By 4th grade they're tired."[4] Although many caring teachers work hard to create nurturing, supportive classrooms, pressure continues throughout school. Some kids feel that no matter how hard they work, there is always more to do. One fifth grader put it bluntly to psychologist Michael Thompson. "I just feel too overwhelmed from work. I never really know what to do. . . . The teachers give kids an undoable amount of work. . . . I get confused everyday."[5] When students feel frustrated in this way, they lose self-confidence. They begin to dislike going to school. What should be an adventure becomes an ordeal.

Middle School Transition

The transition from elementary school into high school is one that many children anticipate eagerly. "It was a lot more fun," seventh graders Colleen, Julia, and Maryanne agreed of their early days in middle school. "We had more freedom." The girls especially liked changing classrooms and getting to know "a different group of kids with each class."[6]

But the challenges of middle school can be daunting as well as exciting. In addition to harder classes, students face increased social pressure in a school that may be much larger than their grade school. New sixth graders are anxious to "fit in," to make new friends, and to show how grown-up they are becoming. Often the desire for popularity outweighs a student's concerns

Teacher Marion Sammartino, now retaired, wrote a column called *School Days*—or, as it was once misprinted, *School Daze*.

about grades. Kids may care more about what their friends think than the assignments in their book bag. If a student's friends value academic achievement, she is more likely to care about her classes. If her group is not interested in school subjects, she may be less interested in working for good grades.

Sooner or later, however, academic demands catch up. According to Sheila Jackson, who works for the school district in Prince George County, Maryland, "The expectations increase in middle school. Kids are expected to manage six or seven classes; they're expected to manage the homework load."[7]

"We're kind of used to it," says seventh grader Maryanne of the one and a half hours worth of homework she and her classmates face most nights.[8] But there are times she wishes she had less to do. For example, one fall afternoon she wanted to play outdoors instead of completing a make-up assignment of five social studies sheets. Julia, who is taking algebra, could also use some extra time to have fun. She feels that thirty problems per night are a lot.

Despite the priority of social concerns in middle school, many kids are already looking to the future. Psychologist William Crain cites an article in which sixth graders freely expressed their anxieties about getting into college. They studied long hours that interfered with their sleep, and they worried about their grades. "It's all being crammed into your brain," one girl complained about the demands of her classes. "It's too much to take."[9]

Tests also become more frequent in middle school, from routine vocabulary quizzes in English to chapter tests in social studies to standardized benchmark tests that determine if students are meeting certain goals. Sports, music, and other activities also compete for after-school time. "I hear [students] talk a lot about being tired because they have so much to do," notes Cynthia Ford, a mother and library media specialist at Midlothian Middle School in Midlothian, Virginia.[10]

Block Scheduling

Block scheduling may help as well as hinder busy students. Instead of attending seven or eight periods a day, students at Midlothian Middle School study their subjects in four blocks of eighty-five minutes. The extended periods give them time to complete some homework at school. But some students would prefer shorter periods. "The day feels very long with only four classes," admits Maryanne.[11] And according to Colleen, classes become almost too intense. "It's too much material to cover in one day," she says.[12]

Another drawback may be that certain classes are only taught for half a year. Students get a double period of social studies one semester and a double period of science another semester. Although technically, they may spend the same number of hours on each subject as they would with a more traditional schedule, the pace of the subject is greatly accelerated. Sometimes it seems as if students are "flying" through the material.

As English teacher Dorene Jorgensen points out, a block schedule can reduce the number of heavy classes kids take at one time. When the plan was instituted at Midlothian Middle School, students took math, English, either science or social studies, and an elective that was not as demanding. That meant no one had more than three hard subjects. Jorgensen considers that a "huge change" from traditional scheduling.[13] Recently, however, she notes that a foreign language has been added at the seventh-grade honors level. This mandatory class ups the number of challenging classes to four.

High School: The Most Well Prepared Students

Most students have another big change when they enter high school. In many ways, they have been prepared for the transition. They are used to having several teachers and to navigating crowded hallways with scarcely a minute to spare. However, the

Homework assignments can sometimes be overwhelming. Many middle schoolers have more than an hour of homework every night.

academic stakes are higher in high school. This is especially true for students aspiring to attend top colleges.

"The standards that create pressure have been raised," explained Bryan Carr, a counselor at James River High School in Midlothian, Virginia. "For high achieving kids, there is more pressure. We have the most well prepared kids in the history of schooling. There's a price for that."[14]

Pressure at All Levels

If the top students are experiencing more pressure, so are students at the opposite end of the spectrum. Minimum requirements for graduation have risen in many schools. More

Selective High Schools

Some public schools are harder than others—and harder to get into. For instance, in Chesterfield County, Virginia, many high schools are classified as specialty centers. By focusing on particular areas such as pre-engineering, the arts, or leadership and international affairs, these schools aim to give interested students a more rigorous grounding in the subject than they would receive at a general high school. But not everyone can attend a specialty school. Students must apply to the specialty center of their choice, almost as if they were applying to college. They must write an essay and get teacher recommendations. Of course, they must also have good grades and take challenging classes in middle school. Although this creates more pressure, for the right student it can be motivating and exciting.

math, science, and social studies may be necessary to earn a diploma.

"One of our biggest problems is what to do if someone fails [a class]," says counselor Gail Hamilton of Oceanside High School in Oceanside, California.[15] In order to graduate, students must take three years of math (including algebra and geometry), one physical science, one biological science, four years of English, three years of social studies, one year of a foreign language, and two years of physical education. These requirements ensure that every graduating student has the background to apply to college.

For those students not as academically inclined as others, this is a very challenging course of study. In the past, a student at Oceanside who failed one class but received passing marks in all his or her other subjects still had enough credits to graduate. This is no longer true since the graduation requirements have been upped to 240 credits. Even with after-school "credit recovery classes" to make up a failing grade, some students are in trouble. "Four years is all you get [to graduate]," explains Hamilton.[16] Students who do not earn sufficient credits may continue to study through the Credit Recovery Center or in summer school. Students who are seventeen or older may attend an evening adult education program at a local junior college. Hamilton said she has seen two students who were 60 credits behind turn everything around and graduate on time. She said that when this happens, "You're looking at a kid going to school from 7:00 A.M. to 9:00 P.M. It's incredible what [such students] can do when they're mature and motivated."[17]

While a great deal of attention is focused on high achievers and on students who are struggling to get by, students in the middle also have to deal with stress. They are the group most likely to be overlooked by concerned counselors and teachers, according to Jennifer Coleman, an assistant principal at James River High School in Midlothian, Virginia.[18] But they, too,

Students hoping to attend top colleges take many challenging courses, such as advanced science classes.

must face hard classes, tests, after-school activities, sometimes hours of homework, and worries about getting into the right college. Many of them are also juggling after-school jobs. Teacher Sarah Mansfield, also at James River High School, says she sees "kids who are spread way too thin" and worries about the effect on them.[19] She attributes a great deal of student anxiety to the SATs. Long before submissions deadlines, the very idea of getting into college causes tension. Aiming high, some students feel that nothing short of perfection will get them into the college of their choice. They place tremendous pressure upon themselves. A high school student named Eve from Faircrest High School in California remarked to educator Denise Clark Pope, "High school is a way of building up a tolerance for stress."[20]

Teachers are not immune to the tension. "The pressure is on educators," admits assistant principal Coleman. "Therefore the pressure is on students. [This] pressure to produce results overshadows the love of learning."[21]

But in spite of everything, no one has to go through school "in a daze." Even while preparing students for standardized tests, most teachers strive to make their subjects interesting and relevant. And many students respond with enthusiasm and curiosity—not all the time, but often enough to give them a sense of adventure. Although some stress is inevitable, students who learn to handle it are preparing themselves for life.

More Sources of Stress

A classic *Peanuts* cartoon, first published in the 1960s, shows Linus complaining to Charlie Brown. He has just received his report card, and his parents and teachers are upset with him. Linus explains that they are disappointed by his grades because they feel he has such potential. Overcome with frustration, Linus wails, "There's no heavier burden than a great potential."[1]

Linus feels that he has let his parents and his teachers down. Like all children, he needs to feel successful, but the adults in Linus's life seem oblivious to his special qualities. Anyone who has thumbed through a collection of old *Peanuts* comics knows that Linus is a deep thinker—even a philosopher. He expresses himself well, and he always has sage advice for Charlie Brown. Linus may not be getting straight As, but there is more than one way to live up to your potential.

Sometimes school policies make children feel as if good grades are the most important or the only way to live up to their potential. Honor rolls in middle schools and high schools list students who received good grades in all their classes. Students may be doing good work—even improving in subjects like reading or math—and still not make the cutoff for the honor roll. For some students, this disappointment looms larger than the very real gains they are making.

While many kids enjoy the challenge that the honor roll presents and the recognition that they receive, too great a focus on academic honors can cause students to stress out over tests and assignments. For a student who has always made the honor roll, the pressure may be intense. Let's imagine a student named Fred. Perhaps the pace of Fred's math class is too rapid for him. He needs more time to assimilate the concepts. Or maybe a history teacher is especially hard in grading papers. But Fred feels he *has* to get good grades. 'What will everyone think if I'm knocked off the honor roll?' Fred worries. He feels that everyone knows him as the smart kid who gets good grades. Like Linus, Fred does not want to let everyone down.

Underachievers and Overachievers

Educators have words for students like Linus and Fred. Students who do not live up to their natural abilities are called underachievers. Those, like Fred, who take hard classes and demand top grades of themselves are classified as overachievers. Sometimes pressured by parents or teachers, they push themselves to excel beyond what comes naturally. Overachievers may sacrifice recreation, sleep, and just plain fun for the sake of good grades.

Some educators do not like the word "overachiever," however.

It seems to subtly undercut a student's accomplishments. "I don't know how you *over*achieve if you're able to achieve," says Bryan Carr, the James River High School counselor.[2]

No one can say that a student is doing too much if that is what the student wants to do. Each must decide what he or she is willing to give up for the sake of grades. In other words, each student must strike his or her own balance. Schoolwork is important, but so are friendships, physical activities, family time, church activities, and a good night's sleep. A student who feels that his or her life has become too heavily weighted down by studies should talk to

> **Students who do not live up to their natural abilities are called underachievers. Those who push themselves to excel beyond what comes naturally are called overachievers.**

a trusted advisor. This can be a parent or family member, a teacher, a counselor, or a close friend. Maybe the student needs to lighten his or her course work or get special help. Maybe he or she needs to play with the family dog after school and take time to practice the guitar. Maybe the student simply needs to relax about academics. Challenges are good, but over-anxiety about grades can only get in the way of learning.

Rewards—Good or Bad?

The honor roll is not the only school benchmark that may increase student stress. At one junior high school in Marysville, California, students who got good scores on an important standardized test received a special treat. They were all invited to party on a Friday afternoon. While two hundred children enjoyed the fun, forty of their classmates were left out. Everyone knew they had not scored well enough to merit an invitation. The superintendent of the school district, Marc Liebman, discussed the policy with a news reporter. "This [the party and similar kinds of rewards] congratulates students on the way they performed and can be a motivator for what they can do this year."[3]

Many educators, however, question the wisdom of a system that rewards the majority and excludes a highly visible minority. Should students be studying so they will be included in a party? Or should learning be its own reward? What about the harshness of excluding students from a fun activity because they did not measure up on a test? Should they be punished for trying and failing? The conclusion some people draw is that incentives such as parties and prizes add to the stress some students may already be feeling.

No More Recess?

An old saying reminds us that everything worthwhile takes time. If someone is writing a play or cleaning a house or examining a patient, more time and effort usually means better results. School administrators know that learning requires lots of time, too. But there are only so many hours in the school day. In an effort to make every moment productive, some grade schools have even done away with recess. Officials reason that reading, math, science, and history are more important than playing. They view recess as a squandering of precious classroom time. According to Alexandra Robbins in her book *The Overachievers: The Secret Lives of Driven Kids*, "At least 40 percent of grade schools across the nation have abolished recess."[4] In fact, some new schools are built without any outdoor play area at all. "We are intent on improving academic performance," explained Benjamin O. Canada in 1998 when he was superintendent of public schools in Atlanta, Georgia. "You don't do that by having kids hanging on monkey bars."[5]

The exact number of grade schools that have cut recess is not known. A 2007 *Time* magazine article states that at least 70 percent of the nation's elementary schools still have recess.[6] But even in schools that do provide recess, some children may be forced to miss it. Kids who are not doing well are sometimes given extra work time while their classmates run outside to play. The idea is that more practice and study will help the students raise their scores.

An organization known as the American Association for the Child's Right to Play (AACRP) hopes to stem the growing trend to do away with recess. According to Audrey Skrupskelis, president of the association, "Recess is getting shorter and shorter because of the push for more 'academic time.' It is seen as an extra that students earn as a reward, rather than as a necessity—a time to unwind, relax, and get the energy out."[7]

Many teachers and parents disagree with the idea that recess

Many elementary schools have eliminated recess in order to give more time to academics, so children miss the chance to get exercise and work off energy.

is an "extra." They believe that recess does more than give kids a chance to stretch their muscles and clear their minds. Recess helps children dissipate stress. It energizes them and enhances their ability to concentrate.[8] "You actually gain instructional time by providing frequent breaks," states Rebecca Lee Lamphere, a lobbyist who seeks to restore recess in the schools.[9] According to writer Christine Gross-Loh, who specializes in natural parenting, "Diminished opportunities for outdoor playtime have been linked with school difficulties, increased childhood anxiety, disconnection from nature, attention deficit disorder, and the epidemic of childhood obesity."[10]

Whose Expectations?

The pressure to succeed academically intensifies in high school. Grades become more important than ever as a requirement for getting into a good college. Caught up in a materialistic society, some students and their parents see education as the key to earning power. These students fear that their whole future life depends on getting into the most prestigious college possible. According to their reasoning, only a degree from an Ivy League university such as Harvard or Yale will guarantee them a top job in the field of their choice.[11]

Although studies show this is not so, competition for spots in the most highly selective colleges remains fierce. Some students choose to load their schedules with the most difficult classes and spend most of their after-school hours doing homework. Other students may find themselves pressured by counselors or parents to take a heavier course load than they desire. They worry that a drop in their grades could have dire consequences when the time comes to apply to college.

Retired teacher and children's author Paul Fleisher believes there are better ways to look at education. "School shouldn't just be preparation for future life," he cautions. "The things you do in school should be of value in and of themselves."[12]

Grades take on a huge significance when kids see them solely as their ticket to a prestigious college or a high-income profession. Psychologist Michael Thompson has talked with many students and parents about their school experiences. He has seen problems arise when parents focus too intently on grades and homework. Speaking as a parent himself, he has written, "When our dreams remain fixed, untempered by our children's reality, our children pay the price."[13]

It is important for students to communicate easily with parents and teachers—especially when they feel they cannot live up to what is being asked of them. No one wants classes to become a burden or compromise students' physical or mental well-being. But a senior at Walt Whitman High School in Bethesda, Maryland, probably spoke for many students when he said, "Everyone is stressed for the simple fact that we're not sure if we're working for our own passion and dreams or for other people's expectations."[14]

The pressure to succeed academically intensifies in high school. Grades become more important than ever as a requirement for getting into a good college.

New Kid at School

Changing schools midyear is never easy. Whether you're six or sixteen, leaving old friends and starting over in a new place can be daunting. "People move around so much," says Joanne Ward, whose daughter Rachel started a new school in the middle of sixth grade. "There's lots of pressure placed on you when you move. That includes academic pressure."[15]

Oceanside High School sees a higher than usual turnover of students. This is because it is situated in Oceanside, California, near the Camp Pendleton Marine Corps base. Many kids from military families attend the school while a parent is stationed at the base or deployed overseas. They are accustomed to moving

Graduation is a time for families to celebrate. But some graduates are not sure whether they are pursuing their own dreams or those of their parents.

around, familiar with the unpredictability of military orders, and used to starting over.

Even so, "Moving to a new school can come at a very inconvenient time," according to Oceanside High School counselor Gail Hamilton.[16] She recalls one young man who attended schools in three states in the course of a single school year. Not only did he have to make the necessary social and academic adjustments, he also had to take standardized tests at all three schools. Because each state sets its own standards, one state is not likely to accept scores from a different test administered in another state.

Hamilton believes that children moving midyear may face challenges on several levels—emotional, social, and academic. It is never easy to start over and find a niche in a new school. Military children, however, may have much greater reason for anxiety. They may be worried about a parent deployed overseas. Concern for a loved one naturally takes precedence over everything else. But support from counselors, teachers, and friends may help students deal with their fears.

Academically, students may find themselves lost in their new classes. Subjects offered at their old school may not be part of the curriculum at the new school. Even when they are able to enroll in the same course, for example, American history, they must adjust to a new teacher, new requirements, and perhaps a new textbook. The emphasis and pace may be different. Where a student may have been studying the Civil War in the previous class, he or she may discover that the new class is already past World War I. Yet the student may be held responsible for the material he or she missed. The student has to work doubly hard to get a good grade and adjust to a new school at the same time.

Anyone who has ever been "the new kid on the block," knows how intimidating it can be. Fortunately there are always students eager to welcome newcomers. Special programs can help, too. Oceanside High School offers a program called "Welcome Aboard Pirates" (the school mascot is a pirate). Old students meet with new students to answer questions and share experiences. Friendships are forged as Oceanside begins to feel like home to the newcomers. Another resource for new students is the Military Child Education Coalition. Founded by a group of military wives, this organization offers support and information to help children transition to their new school.

Whether a student comes from a military family, it is a good idea for him or her to get as much information as possible about a new school before the move. That way there will be fewer disappointments or surprises. Changing schools midyear is a challenge. With a little planning and determination, it can also be a rewarding experience.

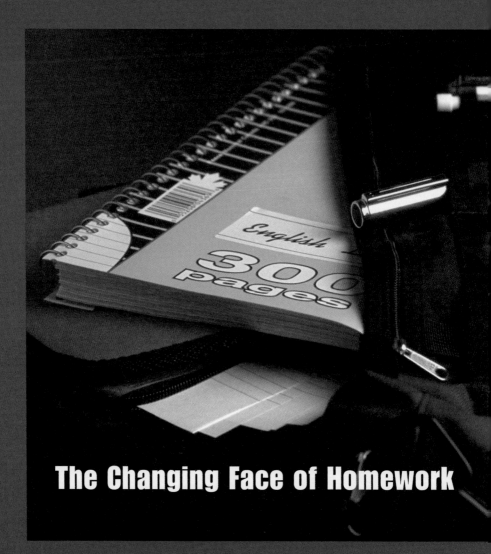

The Changing Face of Homework

Sixth grader Zachary VanDerwerker had a heavy load to carry. His backpack, crammed with books and papers, weighed forty-one pounds. As Zachary struggled to climb the steps to the school bus, the weight of his backpack dragged him backward. He fell off the bus onto the ground. Luckily, Zachary was not badly hurt. However, the U.S. Consumer Product Safety Commission points out that many young people do suffer serious injuries. In 2001, twelve thousands students age seventeen and under strained or sprained muscles due to the weight of their backpacks.[1] Medical treatment for each student cost around $11,000.[2]

Of course, heavy book bags mean lots of homework. Zachary's mother, Mickey VanDerwerker, believes that many students face too much school pressure. She thinks the four hours of homework her son had to do each night in sixth grade was too much. His academic load made it hard for him to enjoy his favorite pastimes and relax.

Most students would list homework as a major cause of academic pressure. It starts at a young age—even first graders are not exempt. In 2001, Karen Alvarez, a first grade teacher in Los Angeles, assigned forty-five minutes a night to the youngsters in her class. "I have such high expectations for these children," Alvarez told a reporter. "I let the parents know that." According to Alvarez, no parents have objected to her strict homework policy.[3] However, plenty of parents besides Jason's and Zachary's mothers do feel that their children have too much homework. They question its usefulness and resent the way that it limits family time.

Crusade Against Homework

The debate over homework is hardly new. In the 1880s, a former Civil War general named Francis Walker became fed up with the amount of homework his children did each night. He felt they were bored, tired, and overly worried about getting everything done. Many parents feel uncomfortable challenging the school system. Walker did not. He was president of the school board in Boston. He convinced the board to limit the amount of homework a teacher could assign.[4]

It was not long before other people took up the crusade against homework. Some doctors claimed that homework kept children cramped indoors for too long. It denied them the benefits of fresh air and exercise. A popular magazine, *Ladies' Home Journal*, also claimed that homework was a threat to good health.

The California legislature took such charges to heart. In 1901, it passed a law that prevented teachers from giving homework to students from kindergarten through eighth grade. The law also set limits on the amount of work that high school kids could be asked to do.[5] Fifteen years later, there was little fuss when the law was revoked.[6]

However, many people continued to battle the concept of homework. In 1930, the American Child Health Association called homework a major factor in rates of tuberculosis and heart disease among young people.[7] A new approach to schooling, the Progressive Movement, broadened the scope of education to include physical and emotional well-being as well as academic achievement. Progressives thought it was more important for children to be healthy and lead well-rounded lives than to master school materials as quickly as possible. One Progressive went so far as to call homework for children in grade school and junior high "legalized criminality."[8]

In 1901, the California legislature passed a law that prevented teachers from giving homework to students from kindergarten through eighth grade.

Despite such opposition, homework did not disappear. Many parents still thought some homework was a good idea. In moderation, homework could help their children become eager and disciplined learners. Teachers continued to hand out some assignments, especially in the upper grades. But according to a national survey, most high school students in 1948 spent less than an hour a night on homework.[9]

Sputnik Changes Education

In 1957, the world entered a new era, the Space Age, with the Soviet launching of the first artificial satellite, *Sputnik 1.* Competition was fierce between the United States and the Communist Soviet Union during the period after World War II

Some students have so many books to carry that their backpacks pose a health danger.

known as the Cold War. Many Americans were shocked and alarmed that the Soviets beat the United States into space. People began to worry that schools in the Soviet Union were turning out better scientists and engineers than American schools. There seemed only one way to remedy this situation. Students would have to study more science and math. To many educators, this also meant that they would have to do more homework.

A Nation at Risk

Even though students were spending extra time on after-school studies, some educators thought they were not doing enough. In 1983, a government publication titled *A Nation at Risk* concluded that children were not being adequately challenged or prepared for the future. The study compared U.S. schools unfavorably with schools in foreign countries. Bluntly it stated that "for too many people education means the minimum work necessary for the moment." Some of the language was even stronger. "If an unfriendly foreign power had attempted to impose on America the mediocre educational performance that exists today," stated the report, "we might well have viewed it as an act of war."[10] Stringent reforms were called for, including more rigorous standards, increased homework, an extended school day, and a longer school year. Schools took the recommendations seriously as the "tougher standards" movement gained acceptance across the country.[11] Teachers began assigning more homework. In 1995, an editorial in a major magazine said that homework was the closest thing possible to "a one word solution to America's educational problems."[12]

In the 1950s, people began to worry that Soviet schools were turning out better scientists and engineers than American schools. There seemed to be only one solution: Students would have to study more science and math.

Continuing Controversy

The debate over homework is not likely to end any time soon. Some educators feel that a strict homework policy is the hallmark of a quality education. Others feel that excessive homework interferes with a child's personal growth. Each child is an individual, they reason. Each has unique emotional and intellectual needs. Demanding the same homework from all students is a misguided attempt to fit all children into a single mold. Which group is correct? The arguments are strong on both sides.

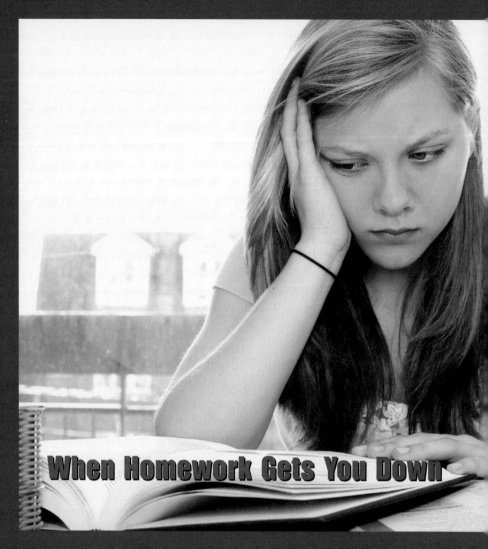

When Homework Gets You Down

The chances are pretty good that if you're in middle or high school, you've got homework tonight. Maybe you're even reading this book as part of a class assignment. But that may not be all you've got to do. You may have a musical instrument to practice or perhaps you play after-school sports. Your younger brother may be clamoring for you to play with him. A friend with a problem may call up, eager to talk. You're making a photo album to surprise your grandma on her birthday. Your scout troop is meeting tonight. You want to go to the mall with your friends. Your pet needs care. The list goes on and on. A myriad of activities compete for your attention, and you have to decide what to do first. Does homework come before everything else? There are certainly many reasons for making homework a top priority.

Benefits of Homework: Worthwhile Challenge

Doing assignments outside of school crams more learning into a single day, argue proponents of homework. It enables students to master material and acquire needed skills more quickly. Tightly packed schedules seldom allot enough time to write a story, solve algebra problems, or research the life of Thomas Edison during the school day. However, these are activities worth doing. Without homework, classes would not be as challenging or rewarding.

Homework also does more than help a student understand his or her studies. According to many educators, it builds character. It teaches students to be persistent and disciplined. It gives them a sense of accomplishment. Students feel proud of a well-written report or proud of solving the problems in a math assignment, and they actually learn more. In this way, homework boosts confidence. It also teaches students to budget time carefully, an essential skill for life in the "real world." Champions of homework say that all these benefits are worth the pastimes students may be forced to sacrifice.

Drawbacks of Homework: Too Much and Too Hard

Can there be too much of a good thing? Most young people would respond with a resounding yes. Almost every student has complained at some time about too much homework. But teachers, eager to present necessary information and skills, keep heaping on assignments. When children have more than one teacher, the problem may be compounded. Their instructors may not coordinate the amount of homework they give. Nobody wants to do twenty math problems and write an English essay the night before a big science test. When assignments pile

The Pluses and Minuses of Homework

On the PLUS side, HOMEWORK . . .

- Enables you to master material more quickly
- Gives you a sense of accomplishment
- Helps build character and gives you a chance to develop determination, persistence, and confidence
- Fosters time management skills
- Helps you get into a good college
- Prepares you to face the rigors of the "real world"

On the MINUS side, HOMEWORK . . .

- Can sometimes be mere "busywork"
- Can cause you to get insufficient sleep
- Leaves you less time for family and social activities
- Creates stress and anxiety
- Can contribute to student burnout
- May not be as effective a learning tool as some teachers think

With some careful planning and a healthy dose of enthusiasm, you can maximize the pluses and eliminate the negatives.

up in this way, homework becomes overwhelming. Students become tense and anxious. They lose the joy of learning and may become resentful if they have to give up activities that they love doing. Parents, called upon to help their children with homework, can also become stymied by the amount and difficulty of homework. "Kids today are overwhelmed," said one frustrated parent. "Schools are pushing too hard and expecting too much from kids."[1]

The Sleep Factor

When students have too much homework, they often lose sleep. The later they stay up, the less alert they become. The next day at school, they are likely to be too tired to concentrate. This is no way for effective learning to take place.

A poll conducted by the National Sleep Foundation in 2004 found that many young children are not getting enough sleep. Although children ages six through ten should get ten to twelve hours of sleep each night, many do not. The situation is even worse for teenagers. More than a quarter of all teenagers fall asleep in school at some time. Many have also fallen asleep doing homework.[2]

"I encourage [my students] not to stay up till 2 or 3 in the morning," says Jeffrey Doyle, who teaches AP world history to sophomores at James River High School, "They still do."[3] But

The National Sleep Foundation warns that many students are not getting enough sleep, particularly high schoolers. Their health and learning may suffer as a result.

by helping kids build the skills they need to succeed academically and making himself available for questions via email, Doyle strives to lessen pressure.

When high school students stay up late to study, they naturally do not feel like getting up in the morning. But there is a second reason they may want to stay in bed. That has to do with their circadian rhythm. Like a form of biological clock, the circadian rhythm dictates when someone sleeps and awakens. As children become adolescents, their circadian rhythm changes so they cannot sleep easily before 11:00 P.M. To get the amount of sleep they need, they have to sleep later in the morning. But this is an impossibility for many teens because their schools start so early.

Congresswoman Zoe Lofgren from California has tried to remedy this situation by introducing a bill, appropriately called the ZZZ's to A Act, into Congress. The measure would encourage high school to delay opening until 9:00 A.M. Schools willing to accept later opening and closing times would receive special funding. Although the proposed legislation has failed to pass Congress several times, Lofgren considers it important enough to keep reintroducing it. "Science has shown us that sleep and achievement are linked," she has stated. "For students to be successful they need their sleep. School hours should mirror adolescents' biological sleep and wake patterns."[4]

> **As children become adolescents, they cannot sleep easily before 11 P.M. To get the amount of sleep they need, they have to sleep later in the morning.**

Later school hours would mean less time at the end of the day for homework, but the gain in student well-being could make the trade-off worth it. In addition, the measure could lessen the risk of students driving while they are exhausted. According to the National Sleep Foundation, 100,000 auto accidents per year are caused by sleep-deprived drivers.[5] Young people between the ages of sixteen and twenty-five account for half of these accidents.[6]

Although most high schools continue to open early, a few have decided to experiment with later hours. Studies indicate that the change paid big dividends in terms of student well-being. More students were able to complete at least part of their assignments at school. Grades tended to go up, while stress levels went down.[7]

Homework Around the World

Many comparisons have been made between American schools and schools in foreign countries. Not surprisingly, one point of comparison has been the amount of homework assigned. According to a study published by two professors from Pennsylvania State University in 2005, American students, especially those in middle school, rank high in the amount of homework they receive. But this does not mean that they score highest on achievement tests. Students in Denmark, Japan, and the Czech Republic spend less time on homework, but receive higher scores. And students in countries that assign a great deal of homework, including Thailand, Iran, and Greece tend to rank behind students who do less homework.[8]

Despite the study's findings, however, few people would argue that homework is all bad. As classes become more demanding in middle and high school, some learning has to take place at home. Some students have a confident attitude toward homework. They expect to get their assignments done and do them well. Other students may be just as capable, but they handle stress poorly. They worry about how much they have to do and yearn for some free time simply to unwind. The challenge is to maximize the good effects of homework and eliminate the bad. Luckily, there are many things that all middle and high school students can do to keep homework from becoming overwhelming. Here are some tips to keep in mind when you're dealing with homework:

Choose courses carefully. Be careful when you're signing up for courses. It is good to challenge yourself, but leave yourself some leeway, too. You do not have to take all the hardest classes. Discuss your class schedule carefully with your counselor and your parents. They will help you decide what is realistic for you. You might want to arrange your day so that you have at least one class that does not require a great deal of daily homework. This could be your chance to try something new, like drama or pottery or music lessons. It could also be an opportunity to unwind and relax in the middle of your school day.

Create a homework game plan. When your teacher gives a homework assignment, pay close attention. Make certain you know exactly what she wants. It helps if you write everything down in a planner. All sorts of these scheduling helpers are available in office supply stores. Choose one with a calendar that leaves plenty of space to write down each day's assignments. Or create your own planning sheets on a computer. Estimate the amount of time you will need for each assignment, and write that down, too. Be generous. Don't plan to write an English essay in ten minutes or build a model of the solar system in the half hour before you go to bed. Be sure to allow yourself plenty of breaks.

Don't wait till the last minute. Putting off your homework as long as possible often backfires. You may run out of time and energy. You may end up cheating yourself on sleep. Or you may end up in class without your homework. The latter situation is not the end of the world, but it can be stressful.

Seek help, if necessary. Almost everyone has trouble with homework at some time or other. As writer and educator Alfie Kohn points out in his book, *The Schools Our Children Deserve,* "No one can learn very effectively without making mistakes and

Asking a friend for help is a good idea for those struggling with an assignment.

without bumping up against limits."[9] Challenging assignments help you to expand the boundaries of your knowledge and skills. Teacher Paul Fleisher explains, "If everything I give them is easy, I'm not doing my job."[10]

> **After you've tried your best and still find a particular assignment challenging, ask for help.**

After you've tried your best and still find a particular assignment too hard, ask a parent, grandparent, older sibling, or classmate for help. If you're still having a problem, do as much of the assignment as you can, then put it out of your mind. Now might be a good time to take a walk, practice a musical instrument, or call a friend. The next day you can explain the situation to the teacher and ask for more help.

Studying for a Test

Not all homework is written, of course. Sometimes when you're studying for a test, it can seem that your homework will never be done. How can you tell when you know enough? Might an extra hour of study make the difference between an A and a B? Test anxiety blows everything out of proportion. It can lessen your concentration and actually make you score lower on the test. One student who suffers from test anxiety explained her frustration to educator and writer Denise Clark Pope:

> When I'm studying I get, like, really very nervous, and then I get a stomachache, and I get so I can't study no more. . . . Then when I get to the test, I fail because I haven't studied! I can't remember anything. I am just blank and can't think.[11]

Another student, now in graduate school, recalls panicking during math tests in high school. "I'd realize I wasn't doing the problems right. It made me physically ill."[12]

If this scenario sounds familiar to you, you should discuss your symptoms with your parents and teacher. There is no need for you to become sick or over-agitated about any test. A counselor may offer techniques to help you relax or to think more clearly under pressure. Perhaps some accommodations can be worked out by allowing you more time for the test or a chance to take a break and walk around.

You can also fight test anxiety by "studying smart"—that is, by organizing your time and materials. You might start by listing the page numbers you need to review and separating the class notes you have to go over. When you know exactly what you have to cover, it will not seem so overwhelming. Concentrate on the major points, then decide what details you should learn. If you start to feel stressed, take a break. Exercise is a good way to break through your apprehension. It is hard to feel negative when you're walking or running or riding your bike. Go into the test relaxed, rested, and ready to do your best.

When the Government Gets Involved

An old saying reminds everyone that two things are inevitable—death and taxes. Some people may well think it is time to add another inevitability—standardized tests. Between September 2005 and June 2006, about 45 million standardized tests were administered in American schools.[1] A tremendous amount of money was spent to see whether students measured up to certain set goals. Teachers worked hard to prepare children academically and psychologically for the tests. Proponents of testing say this is the only way to ensure that all children are getting a quality education. Opponents argue that something vital is lost from education when too much time and effort is expended on meeting state requirements.

Reforming Education

Standardized tests have not always had such overwhelming importance. Much of today's preoccupation with standardized testing dates back to the 1983 publication of *A Nation at Risk*. The scathing indictment of American education shocked elected officials and business people across the country. Something had to be done to get the nation's schools back on track. Should each state define the standards its schools were expected to meet? Some governors and state legislatures began to consider the idea.

Albert Shanker, president of a national teachers' union and a weekly newspaper columnist, also liked the idea of educational standards. He thought it made sense for educational experts to decide what children should be learning in each grade.[2] All schools would have the same requirements for its students. Standards would dictate at what level students should be reading or what math skills they should master. From grade school on up, specific goals would be planned and organized. No one would graduate from high school without a solid education.

In 1990, Maryland became the first state to establish such a system. One year later the state instituted a test to be taken by students at various levels.[3] Soon other states followed suit. The era of widespread standardized tests had begun.

National Goals

Many people found the idea of educational standards appealing. One of them was President George H.W. Bush. In September 1989, he invited state governors to a two-day educational summit meeting. The assembled officials, under the leadership of Arkansas governor Bill Clinton, gave the go-ahead to the

Global Competition

Many people who are dissatisfied with the country's educational system raise some hard questions. What kind of world will today's children live in as adults? Is their education preparing them to flourish in that world? Is it preparing them to uphold America's position as a leader among nations? The National Center on Education and Economy is a nonprofit organization that recommends educational policies to ensure that the United States maintains its competitive edge in the global economy.

In a report released in 2007, the organization found room for a great deal of improvement. "Thirty years ago, the United States could lay claim to having 30 percent of the world's population of college students," states the report.[4] "Today that proportion has fallen to 14 percent and is continuing to fall." Furthermore, continued the report, studies showed that American students were falling behind many foreign countries in science, mathematics, and general literacy.[5] According to the report, this state of affairs could have far-reaching consequences:

> If we continue on our current course, and the number of nations outpacing us in the education race continues to grow at its current rate, the American standard of living will steadily fall relative to those nations, rich and poor, that are doing a better job. If the gap gets to a certain—but unknowable—point, the world's investors will conclude that they can get a greater return on their funds elsewhere and it will be almost impossible to reverse course.[6]

In other words, the United States will cease to be a top nation in the world economy if significant improvements are not made in the American education system. Not everyone agrees with this assessment, of course. Many educators and parents feel that education is about an individual's development—not about economic growth.

creation of educational goals for the entire nation.[7] Since these goals would be voluntary, the states could decide for themselves whether to adopt them. However, there was little for an educator to oppose. Entitled "Goals 2000," the educational objectives were very broad. One stated that "by the year 2000, all children will start school ready to learn." Another said that when the school year was over, all fourth, eighth, and twelfth graders would show "competency over challenging subject matter" and be able "to use their minds well."[8]

After Bill Clinton was elected president in 1992, he continued to push for educational reform. In his State of the Union address in 1997, he called for a program of Voluntary National Tests for fourth grade reading and math.[9] Reaction was mixed, but many people saw a danger in his proposal. "National testing would do nothing to give children a better education or teach them knowledge and skills," according to public figure Phyllis Schlafly.[10] Other commentators foresaw problems with the writing and administration of such tests. They feared that politics would play an inappropriate role in the process.

No Child Left Behind

George W. Bush, who was inaugurated president in 2001, had no such fears. What he did have was a twenty-eight-page proposal for improving the nation's educational system. As the former governor of Texas, Bush knew a great deal about schools and standardized tests. He felt that tests were the best way to judge how well or how poorly schools were doing their jobs. He wanted the results to be tabulated so that schools could track the progress of minority students and low-income children. Children in such groups often scored below their more affluent classmates. Bush wanted to make certain that all children got an excellent education and met certain goals. Schools whose students did not make yearly gains would have to institute improvements. But if their changes did not result in higher test scores, the schools would lose federal funding. If scores continued to lag behind acceptable standards, eventually the school could be shut down.

Ultimately, 90 percent of the country's senators and representatives voted for Bush's plan. On January 8, 2002, he signed the No Child Left Behind Act into law. "As of this hour, America's schools will be on a new path of reform, and a new path of results," he declared.[11]

Although the law includes many provisions, the most

important one stipulates that all children in grades three through eight be tested yearly in reading and math. Each state adopts its own exams. Students have to be tested at least once in high school. The fate of every school and its staff depends on whether test scores show "adequate yearly progress" (AYP). Each new class is expected to show improvement over previous classes. For example, this year's third graders must score higher than last year's third graders by a minimum amount. The goal is for every child to pass the tests by 2014.

Gains in Achievement

Advocates of the No Child Left Behind Act say that it motivates both teachers and children. Teachers focus on the most important things children need to learn. Students work hard to pass the tests. Children make giant leaps in knowledge and skills as evidenced by their high test scores. The students in Stanton Elementary School in Philadelphia, Pennsylvania, have been put forth as an example. Only three years after the enactment of the law, the number of students reading at the level deemed acceptable by the state rose from fewer than two out of ten to seven out of ten.[12] "We've made tremendous progress in helping more and more students get the education they deserve," said Secretary of Education Margaret Spellings. "Numerous independent reports confirm that students are improving, and the long-standing achievement gap [between minority and white children] has begun to close."[13]

Critics of No Child Left Behind

Are tests really the way to ensure that all students receive a quality education? No, reply the critics of the No Child Left Behind Act. They believe there are more effective things that schools can do to help students learn. One of the most important is to reduce class size. Smaller classes mean students get more

Standardized testing is an important part of the No Child Left Behind Act.

individual attention. The teacher can respond more readily to each student's questions and developmental needs.

Of course, smaller classes mean that schools need more teachers. Unfortunately, many bright young people overlook teaching when choosing a career. While teachers have a huge responsibility, they often make less money than people in other professions. Raising their salaries would help attract a larger number of creative and enthusiastic individuals to the field, advocates say.

The lack of creative freedom in many classrooms may also discourage people from going into teaching. Punitive measures enacted against low-performing schools place a great deal of pressure on the principal and teachers. Their jobs and government funding for the school depend on how well students perform on standardized tests. In their anxiety, teachers may restrict their lessons to materials covered on the test. This is known as "teaching to the test." One grade school principal put it simply: "What gets taught is what gets tested."[14] Some schools have cut way back on subjects like art, music, and P.E. Even subjects that are considered more academic, such as history, science, and geography, have been curtailed in some places. This trend deprives children of a great deal of basic knowledge as well as enriching experiences. As one teacher remarked, "How are we going to have informed citizens if they never learn social studies?"[15]

One Size Does *Not* Fit All

Joanne Ward, mother of two college students and a daughter in middle school, feels that students are shortchanged by the emphasis on standardized tests. "The teachers literally review and teach to the tests. What do these [tests] prove?" she asked.[16]

In some school districts, teachers are told not only *what* to teach but *when* to teach it. Pacing charts tell them exactly what lesson to present on what day. Bound to a strict schedule, teachers have no time to pursue interesting topics that might arise during a class discussion. State standards rather than children's curiosity dictate the lesson plans.

Not surprisingly, many teachers object to this situation. "The most important idea in education," according to retired teacher Paul Fleischer, "is that you teach to the individual child." But pacing charts impose a "one size fits all" mentality on the classroom. All children are expected to learn at the same rate. "If students don't fully understand a certain concept, they are not ready to move on," says Fleisher. "But the pacing charts dictate that the teacher must move on."[17]

Mickey VanDerwerker, a teacher, mother of five, and school board member in Bedford, Virginia, is also unhappy with the restriction placed on educators. "Teachers are given scripts and told exactly what to cover," she says. "[They] do the same thing every day in every school. [They] can't improvise. Kids are missing out on the spontaneity that used to exist in classes."[18]

When Spontaneity Flourishes

Educator Marion Sammartino agrees that children are the losers when teachers are forced to abdicate freedom and creativity. She recalls a memorable activity from the 1970s, a time when spontaneity flourished in her school district. The project grew out of an unanticipated discussion in an eighth grade social studies class. The students were discussing the ways in which their lives differed from those of their parents and grandparents when they were young. The students were obviously enjoying swapping tales, and Sammartino chose not to interrupt their enthusiasm. Instead, by the end of the period, she had thought of a way to harness it. The students embarked on a unit dubbed "The Yesteryears of Oceanside," in which they studied the history of their hometown of Oceanside, California. Because there had been little written about the topic, they interviewed senior citizens. The students learned the importance of oral history, wrote up their interviews in a booklet, and made a videotape that won an award from the city.

In some school districts, teachers are told not only what to teach but when to teach it. Bound to a strict schedule, teachers have no time to pursue topics that might arise during class discussion.

"It was a wonderful experience," remembers Sammartino. "The kids got to learn history from people instead of textbooks. They learned that history isn't just something that happened long ago and far away. History is an ongoing process, and, in our own way, we are all a part of it." Marion Sammartino, however, wonders whether she would be able to create a similar unit in today's educational climate. "It wouldn't fit in with state standards or prepare kids for tests," she said. "But it did teach them a lot and get them awfully excited about history."[19]

Moms Fight Back in Virginia

Creativity, curiosity, enthusiasm, and joy in learning are not qualities that can be measured on a test. Yet these are important traits for success in school and in life. Critics of "No Child Left Behind" fear these are the very characteristics being thwarted by a relentless emphasis on standardized tests. Other educators point to rising test scores as a sign that American schools are improving. They reason that children must be getting a quality education if they continue to do well on tests.

Mickey VanDerwerker disagrees. "Kids aren't smarter," says the educational activist and former Teacher of the Year. "They're better at taking tests."[20] She questions the depth of their knowledge of the material on which they're tested.

Several years ago VanDerwerker and about twenty other mothers founded an organization to reform standardized testing in Virginia. Even before the No Child Left Behind Act, students in Virginia were required to take Standards of Learning (SOL) tests. Instituted in 1998, these tests in reading, math, and other subjects are based on curriculum requirements set by the State Department of Education. In order to graduate from high school, students must pass a certain number of SOL tests. The state also requires SOL scores to be a factor in the promotion of students in third, fifth, and eighth grades.

> Creativity, curiosity, enthusiasm, and joy in learning are not qualities that can be measured on a test. Yet these are important traits for success in school and in life.

The group that VanDerwerker helped establish, Parents Across Virginia United to Reform the SOLs, or PAVURSOL, does not oppose standards or testing. But the members feel that test results should not be overemphasized. They believe that "local teachers and principals, rather than the state, should set the standards."[21] They do not want programs such as art, music, and recess eliminated to make more time for test preparation.

Their mission statement also stipulates that no "major educational decisions" should be based solely on SOL scores. In addition, PAVURSOL members want to ensure that "low-income, minority, [and] disabled children" do not suffer any discrimination.[22]

Merely Tools

Virginians are not alone in their opposition to an excessive dependence on standardized testing. According to one survey, seventy-eight percent of the nation's teachers feel that the No

Some teachers object to the No Child Left Behind Act because they say it has resulted in "teaching to the test" and has caused cutbacks in important programs.

Child Left Behind Act needs to be modified.[23] An even higher percentage, eighty-five, believe that standardized test scores receive too much emphasis.[24] Most teachers believe that there are other important ways to gauge academic progress. Standardized tests are merely tools. They should not be the major goal of the school year.

Many children have bigger concerns than how well they do on a test. Elementary school teacher Jane Chapin recalls coaching a girl for her SOL test in Virginia. The child was deeply concerned about the health of her grandmother, who was her primary caregiver. She had little interest in practicing her test-taking skills. During the coaching session she broke into tears, repeating her worries over and over. Not surprisingly, she did poorly on the test. School administrators, who knew nothing about the child's personal life, could only focus on her low SOL scores. Instead of seeing the whole child, pressured officials saw only a set of numbers.

David Elkind had some things to say about the growing emphasis on tests almost thirty years ago:

> Management programs, accountability, and test scores are what schools are about today and children know it. They have to produce or else. The pressure may be good for many students, but it is bound to be bad for those who can't keep up. Their failure is more public and therefore more humiliating than ever before. Worse, students who fail to achieve are letting down their peers, the principal, the Superintendent, and the school board. This is a heavy burden for many children to bear and is a powerful pressure to achieve early and to grow up fast.[25]

Test Anxiety Revisited

Despite such views, the importance of standardized tests is conveyed to students over and over. In some schools they are primed like athletes prior to a big game. Their opponent is the test; their job is to conquer it. They are drilled continuously.

They take one or more practice tests. In some places, they even sing pep songs. Under these circumstances, it is common for even well prepared students to feel some nervousness. Students less likely to do well may be considerably more agitated. In a few instances, overly anxious children have vomited on their tests. Teachers are instructed to seal such tests in plastic bags and send them on to be scored.

Tension before a big test may be a bit like stage fright. Most actors say that some stage fright is normal and that it actually enhances their performance. Too much stage fright, however, has the opposite effect. It may paralyze the actor, cause him to mumble lines, miss cues, or focus on the audience instead of the characters on stage. In the same way a little anxiety before a test may help keep you mentally alert. Too much apprehension can block your ability to concentrate, making it difficult for you to remember things.

The importance of standardized tests is conveyed to students over and over. In some schools they are primed like athletes prior to a big game.

There is a biological basis for this phenomenon. Author and educator Leslie Hart has studied the human brain and concluded that excessive anxiety impairs a student's ability to learn. Excessive stress causes a person's brain to "downshift."[26] This means that the brain cannot process information as effectively. According to authors and researchers Renate Nummela Caine and Geoffrey Caine, students should aim for "relaxed alertness."[27] Such a state of mind, calm but eager, frees students to do their best work.

Besides studying for a test, it is a good idea for students to prepare physically and psychologically. They should get plenty of sleep the night before and eat a good breakfast. It is also wise not to keep studying or talking about the test up until the last possible moment. This helps a student clear his or her head and go into the test with a calm attitude.

If students find themselves stressing out in the middle of a test, they should take a few deep breaths. It can help to take a moment to put things in perspective. Anyone who starts to feel ill should tell a teacher.

Tests are merely tools. They measure knowledge but not what a student will do with that knowledge. They do not predict the enthusiasm or imagination that any individual will bring to his or her future.

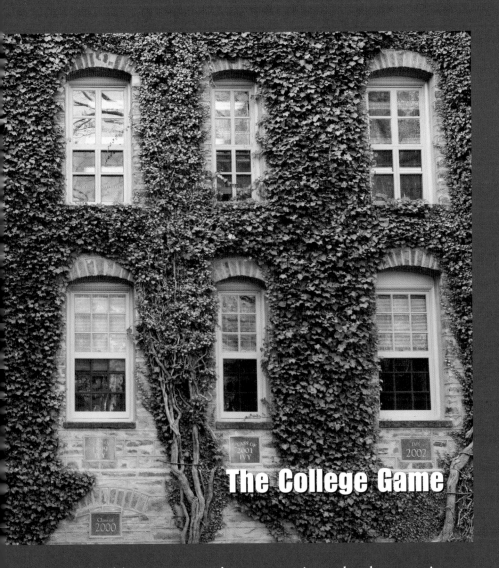

The College Game

You probably are not used to comparing school to an airport. But pediatrician and educational specialist Mel Levine sees a connection that might surprise you.[1] At the conclusion of his bestselling book, *A Mind at a Time*, Levine explains that students come from many different backgrounds just as the passengers at an airport come from many different places. They are all going to different places, too. The passengers at an international airport may wind up anywhere from Mexico City to London to Tokyo. If you think of your classmates as fellow passengers, try to imagine what their destinations might be. After graduation, they may scatter all over the country. Some may travel to foreign countries. Interests and career paths will take them in many different directions, too. Students from your school will become musicians and engineers, auto mechanics and businesspeople, teachers and gardeners and dozens of other occupations. Not all of these goals require college. Some students may be quite content to let their formal education end with their graduation from high school. As Levine has written, he has "met plenty of successful adults who never attended college."[2]

There are many reasons why other students decide to go to college. Preparing for a future career is only one. A college education gives someone a chance to sample different academic disciplines. It helps him or her acquire self-awareness and knowledge of the world. College experiences in and out of the classroom may help a person decide what to do with his or her life.

Getting into a prestigious college is the dream of many high school students. It is a dream often carefully nurtured, sometimes even instilled, by their parents. The problem, of course, is the number of applicants to the nation's top colleges and universities. More students want to go to big name schools than the schools have slots available. As we have seen, some students feel they have to do everything perfectly to win one of those slots. They must take the hardest classes and get all As. They must take part in a broad spectrum of extracurricular activities, including sports and student government. Their SAT scores must be astronomical, their class ranking number one, their college essays polished and flawless.

Students who demand perfection of themselves are certain to feel overburdened at some time. All the hype surrounding college admissions does not help matters. Books abound on how to apply to college. Special courses promise the skills to ace entrance exams. Private counseling companies (which can charge many thousands of dollars) offer to help students present

The need to do well on tests in preparation for college is a source of anxiety for many students.

themselves in the best light to college admissions officers. College rankings in news magazines generate increased applications for the top-rated schools.

While some tension is inevitable, college-bound seniors do not have to focus all their energy on the application process. There are many college options available for students of varied academic records. These are fine institutions that offer a wide array of opportunities. The challenge and excitement comes in finding the college that is a right match for you.

Class Rankings and Grades

College applications take competition to a whole new level. According to writer Alexandra Robbins, 81 percent of public high schools rank students according to their grade point average (GPA).[3] Since class ranking is used to determine the valedictorian and salutatorian, some students place great value on where they fall in the class hierarchy. They want the recognition of being number one as well as the advantage they feel that this will give them in the college application process. But the difference between number 1 and number 2, or number 29 and 30 for that matter, can be as little as one thousandth of a point.[4]

In their frenzy to achieve number one class ranking, some students and their families have even resorted to lawsuits. In 2003, a high school senior in Michigan sued his school district when he was not ranked number one in his class. The student had received special credit for working in a law office. He claimed he should have received an A plus instead of an A for his experiences. The student's mother, who also worked at the firm, backed him up, saying that the work he did "was what he would do if he were a paralegal in a law office. He prepared documents, met with clients."[5] Another student in Texas sued after she missed being named valedictorian by .00154 of a point.[6] In both instances, the students won their lawsuits.

Of course, most people would argue that a miniscule fraction of a point or the difference between a number one and number two class ranking is not significant. Students ranked below the top ten or twenty percent can still have excellent grades and be considered high achievers. These lawsuits show the intensity of the pressure that some students are feeling. They feel they must do something extraordinary to make themselves stand out among thousands and thousands of college applicants. In reality, however, a small difference in class ranking is unlikely to make any difference in the college admission process.

College Entrance Exams

One hurdle many students especially dread, as they apply to college, is facing the exams that most college applications require. The best known is the SAT Reasoning Test (formerly known as the Scholastic Aptitude Test or the Scholastic Assessment Test). Called by Alexandra Robbins "the most feared test in the United States," the SAT is supposed to measure aptitude or potential for learning.[7] Other tests called SAT Subject Tests (formerly known as achievement tests or SAT IIs) measure how much a student has learned in a particular subject like chemistry or French. Of course, everyone wants to do as well on these tests as he or she can. Most students sign up to take the PSAT (the preliminary test) in their sophomore year. This gives them an idea of how well they will do on the actual test in their junior year. If the score is disappointing, there is time to figure out what went wrong and to practice the different kinds of verbal and math questions before taking the test again. Some students find special preparation classes helpful, but these classes certainly are not essential to scoring well. Even if the final score is not what the student hoped for, there are still many good schools ready to consider his or her application. The SAT is simply one of several criteria college admissions officers use to get to know applicants.

Admissions officers at some colleges are beginning to say they do not need scores to figure out if their college is right for a particular student. Although most schools (according to *Newsweek*, the exact number is 88 percent) still require some form of entrance exam, a sizeable minority have made such tests optional.[8] George Mason University in Virginia is willing to accept students who have not taken the SAT, although there are certain restrictions on the test-optional policy. If an applicant to George Mason decides not to take the test, he or she must get extra recommendations as well as write an extra essay. For students who do not test well or have test anxiety, the trade-off is well worth it. Andrew Flagel, the dean of admissions at George Mason, hopes the policy will help alleviate the stress many high school seniors feel. "If you know there are schools out there where it's not going to make a difference, then it's not a high-stakes test," he told *Newsweek*. "And if it's not a high-stakes test, maybe you can relax a little. And maybe you do better."[9]

Senior Year Stress

College-bound students must cram a great deal into the first semester of their senior year. Most college applications are due by the end of the calendar year. It is time to make some hard decisions. To which colleges should the students apply? How many applications are necessary? What about financial aid? Should they apply for early decision at their top choice? Early decision, increasingly popular among some students, lets an individual know whether he or she has been admitted to a college several months before the general pool of applicants receives such information. If a student is accepted, he or she is obliged to attend that college. Someone who is not accepted early may have their application deferred. This means he or she will be considered again with other candidates.

Completing the applications is time-consuming. Some students may also be boning up to take the SAT a second or even third time. Meanwhile, school does not stop just because some seniors are applying to college. Although the junior year is generally considered the toughest, seniors face heavy course loads that may include calculus, physics, and advanced language and history classes. Colleges will want to see the grades they get in these courses before making final decisions.

"The pressure is crazy," said a student at Stuyvesant High School in New York City.[10] An especially rigorous public school, Stuyvesant is selective in its student body. Students must apply for admission. Virtually all students at Stuyvesant go on to college, most aiming for prestigious institutions.

Competition among students is keen. An editorial in the school newspaper sums up the strain, almost frenzy, that some Stuyvesant seniors experience. "In the midst of AP's and college applications, many students have a hard time finding the meaning to it all. Classes are just taken for the grades, and those only for the application to an Ivy League university."[11]

Good News

If college applications are beginning to sound scary, there is plenty of good news to counteract student anxiety. The best is that there are many fine colleges actively recruiting students. These institutions may not have instant name recognition, but they provide a good education and produce happy and successful graduates. If a student wants to go to college and is willing to work hard, he or she is almost certain of being accepted in college. Working hard does not mean a student has to take all AP classes or have a straight A average. No one has to be a super-student, juggling several extra curricular activities after school and arriving home exhausted. It is not even necessary to be one of the top-ranked students in the senior class or make the honor roll every semester. All of these are wonderful accomplishments that may lead to a prestigious college. However, if a student's goal is simply to get a good education at a solid institution, he or she can relax a bit. "We are well able to meet the needs of all of our children who want to go to college," affirms guidance counselor Bryan Carr.[12] A student's future does not depend on attending one of the so-called Ivy League schools.

Journalist Jonathan Alter also feels that too much emphasis is placed on elite institutions to the exclusion of many fine schools. According to his "300 school" model, "students can attend any of 300 or so colleges and receive a terrific education."[13] Alter acknowledges the number of excellent schools may be closer to 500 or even 1,000. Whatever the figure, no student should feel inadequate for failure to be admitted to one of the big name schools. The future is still bright. Everyone should approach high school and college studies with a sense of adventure and a determination to make the most of his or her education.

Writing the Application

Senior year should be a time for fun as well as work. Although a certain amount of tension may be inevitable in applying to college, a few guidelines may help minimize your stress.

Give yourself choices. Discuss with your parents and guidance counselor what you hope to get out of college. It is not unheard of for students to apply to a dozen or more colleges. This may lead to more options, but it is a big job. And it is not necessary. A good rule of thumb is to divide your applications among three kinds of schools. Start with one or two "stretch" (or "reach") schools. These are highly competitive colleges where your chances of acceptance are smaller than at some other good places. That is why they are called "stretch" schools. Your admission is something of a stretch or a long shot. But if a particular school appeals to you, do not be afraid to apply. You may get in after all. Even if you do not, you'll know that you did your best.

If you like, you may skip "stretch schools" altogether. The next applications are for schools that will likely accept you—strong possibilities. Counselors at James River High School in Midlothian, Virginia, call these "competitive schools."[14] Your GPA and test scores are comparable to those of students already in attendance, so you are "competitive" with them.

Finally, you should not neglect what are sometimes called "safety net" or just "safety" schools. These are colleges that are certain to take you. Having a "safety net" takes some of the worry out of the application process. These schools can provide an excellent education. So can community colleges. These local institutions accept everyone with a minimum GPA. Students

Deciding which colleges to apply to can be a grueling process. Experts say it's a good idea to consider different types of colleges—"stretch," "competitive," and "safety" schools.

can live at home and save money if they opt for a community college. When they graduate with an AA (Associate of Arts) degree, they may apply to four-year colleges or look for jobs.

Don't succumb to peer pressure. This is not the time to compete with classmates. It is natural to talk about college with your friends, but try to avoid comparisons. One student's "reach school" may be another student's "competitive school." An especially outstanding student may include schools in his or her "safety net" that others have placed on their "reach" list. Your guidance counselor will help you decide what is realistic for you. Whatever your choices, attack the application process with enthusiasm. Don't feel pressured to apply to a big-name school simply because some of your friends may be doing so. What is right for them may not be what is right for you.

Keep a calendar. Note the date when each of your applications is due. Create your own deadlines in advance of these. Decide when you want to have a first draft of your college essays done. Write that down as well as appointments you make with your English teacher or counselor to go over the essays. Then note when you want each individual essay to be complete. Give yourself a "due date" for each aspect of your applications. Be sure to allot yourself plenty of time, and be realistic about all the other things you have to do. Scheduling your applications in this way will make the whole job of getting into college feel more manageable. When the last application is mailed, you can celebrate.

Don't expect to get into every college on your list. Of course, it is disappointing to receive a rejection letter. But many factors come into play when admissions officers are choosing future students. There are some factors you have no control over such as the school's directive for geographic or ethnic diversity. And it is often difficult to get into a popular state school like the University of Virginia or one of the University of California campuses if you do not live in that state.

Not gaining admittance to a particular college does not mean that you are less capable or that you will be less successful than the students who were admitted. Many famous individuals recall not being admitted to top name universities. These include senator and former presidential candidate John Kerry and Meredith Veiera, co-host of the morning TV show *Today,* who were both rejected by Harvard.[15] Mother and educator Mickey VanDerwerker puts things in perspective when she says, "It's not so much where you go to school [that counts] as what you take with you."[16]

Negative Fallout from Stress

Wilbur and Orville Wright knew a thing or two about pressure. If they hoped to get a heavier-than-air flying machine off the ground, everything had to be perfect. Their very lives could be at stake. Even more than psychological pressure, the brothers had to deal with the physical reality of air pressure. It is air pressure pushing against the undersides of an airplane's wings that enable the craft to fly.

Identical airplanes require the same amount of pressure (or "lift") in order to fly. However, there is no such thing as totally identical people—not even twins. Each person experiences pressure a little bit differently. Some have a low tolerance for academic stress. Juggling assignments, even simple ones, becomes anxiety provoking. The more these students have to do, the more nervous they become. Other students have a much higher tolerance for stress. It sharpens their efficiency and perhaps gives them a competitive edge. High or low, everyone has a level at which stress begins to exert a negative rather than a positive effect.

Too much pressure extracts a physical and mental toll. People may cry or become angry more easily. They may suffer from headaches or stomachaches. People have even been known to suffer temporary hair loss due to intense psychological pressure. Students are not immune to the serious consequences of stress. Four destructive results of intense academic pressure are burnout, cheating, eating disorders, and substance abuse.

Burnout

No one can work at peak efficiency all the time. Everyone needs some "down time" to relax, listen to music, or do anything or nothing at all. The hectic pace of modern education and after-school commitments makes this almost impossible for some students. Every minute is structured or spoken for. When an eighth grader or tenth grader has no chance to unwind, school may seem like a burden with no relief in sight. It is hard to stay motivated under such circumstances. Somehow school no longer seems worth the effort. Faced with a mountain of homework, the student may feel paralyzed. The effort required to complete all his or her tasks no longer seems worth it. This condition is called burnout.

A student suffering from burnout is likely to let schoolwork slide. Worse than that, however, the student has lost enthusiasm for learning. Mel Levine says that some students may lose their incentive when a particular task "takes too much time and energy."[1] Instead of feeling challenged, they feel overwhelmed. Their tolerance for stress decreases, and they may become depressed. Their mantra becomes, "School is full of useless stuff that they make you learn."[2]

Depression has become all too common in modern society. Adults and younger people suffering from depression may experience fatigue and a loss of interest in things they formerly enjoyed. They may feel sad and dread facing the day. Routine jobs or schoolwork may loom as almost formidable tasks. It is not easy to get over depression or burnout alone. But there is always help available. If intense pressure has caused you to lose your motivation, the following guidelines may help you on the road back to your former, more energetic self.

Remember you are not alone. Many students have felt exactly as you do. They have managed to complete their classes successfully and regain their energy. You can too!

When stress is too great, burnout can occur. Students can lose their motivation and interest in learning and school activities.

You do not have to be a super-student. It is better to be healthy and happy than to get straight As. "If you don't get an A, that doesn't mean you're not capable," points out English teacher Autumn Nabors.[3]

Share your feelings with an adult you trust. This could be a parent, counselor, or therapist. Explain that you cannot muster your old interest in your classes, and you wonder if the effort you put out is really worth it. Sometimes just talking about a problem makes you feel better. You'll probably receive sound advice, too. Tell your teacher if you've fallen behind in her class or do not think you can complete an assignment on time. Perhaps certain adjustments can be made. Find someone to help you plan a schedule that gives you time for yourself as well as time to get your schoolwork done.

Keep moving. Exercise stimulates the brain and goes a long way toward restoring optimism and reducing anxiety.

Meditate. When you feel anxious or burdened, take some time to center yourself. Breathe slowly and deeply. You might want to quietly repeat affirmations such as "I am a special person with unique gifts and talents." Or, "I recognize joy and friendship in my life." Listening to soothing music might also be helpful. Find what works for you.

Eat well. Schoolwork may be important. But your health and well-being are more important. When hunger strikes, reach for natural foods instead of preprocessed snacks. Fresh fruits and vegetables are good for your body and increase your energy. It is also important to eat plenty of protein to keep your brain functioning at high efficiency.[4]

Don't stint on sleep. The old maxim "Everything looks better in the morning" is true only if you've had enough sleep. When you're exhausted, everything seems overwhelming. But when you're rested, it is easier to muster enthusiasm for the tasks ahead of you.

Cheating

Everyone knows that cheating is wrong. No matter the pressure or workload a person faces, there is always an alternative to cheating. But some studies indicate that cheating is on the rise in middle and high schools. A disturbing statistic published by the Carnegie Foundation in 2004 indicates that about two thirds of high school students have cheated on a test. The figure jumps to 90 percent when it comes to homework.[5]

According to one survey conducted in 1998, there seemed to be more cheating in schools that focus a great deal of attention on the honor roll and good grades.[6] Sometimes even a student who has proved dependable and trustworthy may resort to cheating. One mother discussing her daughter's dishonesty on a standardized test commented, "She was so worried about doing well on the test that she cheated." The child was only eight years old.[7]

The mistaken idea that your high school performance will determine your success in life places enormous stress on students. "The better grades you have, the better school you get into, the better you're going to do in life," explained one student. "And if you learn to cut corners to do that, you're going to be saving yourself time and energy. In the real world that's what's going to be going on. The better you do, that's what shows. It's not how moral you are getting there."[8]

Of course, many people disagree and think that morality is vastly important. There is certainly more to a fulfilling life than academic, financial, or professional success. Most students find it hard to feel good about themselves when they have cheated. There are practical considerations, too. Academic dishonesty leaves the cheater less prepared to deal with the educational challenges he or she will meet down the road. If a student cheats on a math exam, for instance, he or she will encounter more difficulty with the next semester's math class. If someone hands in an English essay or a history report that is not his or her own, that student is likely to have trouble with future papers he or she is assigned to write. A frequently asked question sums up the dilemma: Would you want to be operated on by a surgeon who cheated in medical school? Cheating robs a student of the chance to develop competence in a given subject or field.

Cheating is also a very risky business. If someone is caught cheating, the consequences are unpleasant. A student who might have received a B or a C without cheating may end up with a failing grade instead. Teachers are getting more skilled at detecting the various ways students may cheat on homework or tests. For example, some students have felt that it is "safe" to use the Internet to purchase papers. This practice even has a name—"cybercheating."[9] But now teachers can submit students' papers to Web sites that check them against comprehensive databases. The Web site lets the teacher know if the paper has been taken from the Internet. Many students have been caught in this way. There is simply no foolproof way to cheat. The threat of being found out will always add to the academic anxiety that the person doing the cheating already feels.

> According to a 1998 study, there seemed to be more cheating in schools that focus a great deal of attention on the honor roll and good grades.

In many ways, cheating is unfair to the person doing it. It is also unfair to classmates who work hard but receive lower grades. After describing various ways some of her classmates have cheated on tests, a girl in high school explained to writer Denise Clark Pope that cheating "screws over the honest students because the teacher never changes the test and grades everyone on the same curve."[10] This hardworking student refuses to take shortcuts herself. Instead she is resolved to "work [her] way to the top the right way, the honest way, by not cheating or cutting class."[11]

Everyone must live with his or her own conscience. Just

because other students may be cheating does not make it right. Despite pressures and deadlines, the best course of action is simply not to cheat.

Eating Disorders

Grades are important, but something else is more important. That is your health. Intense academic pressure can contribute to an already existing tendency to an eating disorder. Anxiety over grades does not cause the disorder, but the tension may make it worse. The main eating disorders that students are liable to develop are anorexia, bulimia, and binge eating (also known as compulsive overeating). Although most students who suffer from eating disorders are young women, sometimes boys are also affected. The National Eating Disorders Association has reported that 10 million women and girls are struggling with anorexia or bulimia.[12]

The excessive emphasis the media places on body image has contributed to an increased rate of anorexia nervosa. Girls who have anorexia worry about getting fat. They limit their food intake drastically, sometimes literally to the point of starving themselves. Even when they are dangerously underweight, they are afraid to eat. Often they feel cold, weak, and may stop having menstrual periods. Among the more serious symptoms are low blood pressure, decreased heart rate, and feelings of weakness.[13] Severe cases may prove fatal.

A number of factors besides body image can increase the likelihood of a person becoming anorexic. These include anxiety, worry, stress, and a desire for perfection. Such characteristics are also associated with academic pressure. Students who feel overwhelmed by their classes or believe they have to be perfect to get into a good college may feel their lives are out of control. In a strange, perhaps unconscious, way, they view eating as something that they *can* control. The sad reality is that once the disease takes over, they have lost control of their eating

Extreme academic stress can contribute to problems such as eating disorders. One is anorexia, in which people with an unrealistic body image severely restrict the food they eat.

habits, too. Impaired health may make it difficult for them to concentrate on their studies. They may fall behind in school-work, increasing their academic stress in a vicious circle.

Young women or men with bulimia eat large amounts of food, often when they're not even hungry. This is called binge-ing. Although bingeing may provide them a momentary relief from the stress in their lives, academic or otherwise, the relief is short-lived. Afterwards bulimics feel nervous and upset about eating so much. Like anorexics, they worry about gaining weight. So they purge themselves of what they have eaten. Usually, this takes the form of vomiting. Once again, the health risks are alarming. Prolonged periods of bulimia can lead to heart problems and kidney damage, osteoporosis, gum disease, and the eroding of the lining of the esophagus.[14] Death may result from extreme cases of bulimia.

Binge eating is another disorder that affects some people. It has been estimated that one quarter of the obese people in the United States are binge eaters. Most, but not all, people who suffer from this eating disorder are obese. For them, eating has become a way to deal with their emotions such as anger, boredom, or anxiety.[15] Academic pressure may also contribute to the disorder. Hunger has little to do with their eating habits. Eating has become a compulsion.

No one should feel ashamed of having an eating disorder. Anorexia, bulimia, and binge eating are medical conditions for which hope and help are available. Sometimes medicine is prescribed in the first two disorders, but counseling is often the best way to overcome an eating disorder. The patient must understand why his or her eating habits have gotten out of control and learn healthy habits to replace them. It takes a good deal of courage and determination to change. Recovery may be a slow, ongoing process, but it is worth the effort to ensure peace of mind and physical well-being.

Substance Abuse

Sometimes academic pressure, in combination with peer pressure, leads students to experiment with alcohol or drugs. This is always a mistake. The very brief respite one may experience from stress is not worth the resulting risks. Even a small amount of alcohol can result in significant impairment. The danger is that the person doing the drinking may not even realize what is happening. Substance abuse may result in fatigue, irritability, headache, and general malaise. Because thinking processes are slowed down for many hours, students are not able to complete homework assignments as rapidly as usual. They find it difficult to concentrate and to learn new material. There is also the very real threat of addiction that can literally take over someone's life. The best policy is to resist the temptation to drink alcoholic beverages or to accept an invitation to try drugs.

What Matters Most

The dangers, both large and small, of intense stress are very real. However, they can he resisted. Teachers, parents, counselors, and ministers are ready to help you if the tension becomes too intense. It also helps to remember that while grades are important, they are not the most important things in the world. Think about what really matters to you most. To gain perspective, teacher Sarah Mansfield encourages students to ask, "In twenty years, what's going to matter? What am I going to remember?"[16]

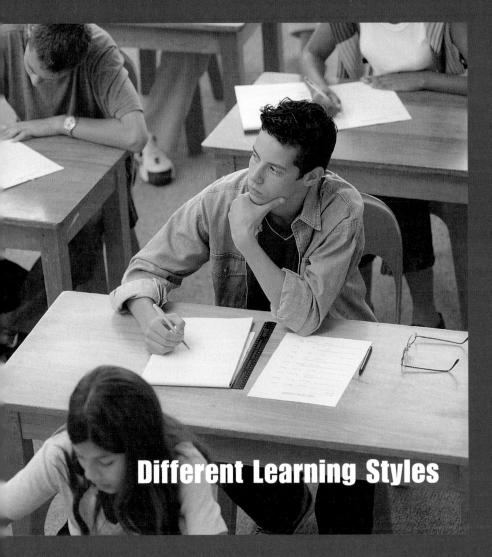

Different Learning Styles

Everyone has his or her own learning style. Sometimes a student's learning style fits in well with the classroom routine. This is not always so. Here is a story about a girl whose learning style caused her a great deal of frustration. Patricia loved stories. She had been eager to read since she started kindergarten, but by the time she was eight years old and in third grade, she still had not learned to read. The other children made fun of her, which made her very unhappy. It took an exceptionally observant and caring teacher to realize that Patricia perceived letters differently from the other children. That meant she needed a different method to learn to read. Her teacher worked hard to provide her with one. Patricia Polacco tells the whole story in her wonderful picture book, *Thank You, Mr. Falker.*[1] You may recognize her as the author of such popular children's books as *Applemando's Dreams*, *Rechenka's Eggs*, and *My Rotten Redheaded Older Brother*. Not only did Polacco overcome dyslexia and learn to read, she also became a fantastic writer and illustrator.

Patricia Polacco is only one of many gifted persons whose learning styles are not receptive to standard instructional methods. Alexander Graham Bell, best known for inventing the telephone, is another such individual. Born in Scotland in 1847, young Alexander was a bright and inquisitive boy. But he did not do especially well in school, and his grades disappointed his father.[2] Later in life he became a terrible procrastinator when he had to write anything. Routine matters bored him. But he wrote, "I have my periods of restlessness when my brain is crowded with ideas tingling to my fingertips when I am excited and cannot stop for anybody."[3] His impulsivity and unusual work habits have led some psychologists to speculate that he might have had what is today called attention deficit disorder, or ADD. Yet no one has ever questioned his genius.

Everyone has his or her own learning style. Sometimes a student's learning style fits in well with the classroom routine, but not always.

Because dyslexia and ADD are classified as disorders, many people feel that there is a stigma attached to them. However, students with learning disabilities are as bright and capable as anyone else. Their brains simply work differently. Everyone, from the top students to those struggling to get by in their classes, has a unique set of strengths and weaknesses. Instead of saying a student has a learning disorder, many psychologists prefer the term "learning difference." This eliminates the idea that something is "wrong" with a student whose learning style does not fit easily with those of his or her classmates.

"By definition, the term difference has a much less negative connotation than disability," say authors Nancy Boyles and Darlene Contadino in *The Learning Differences Source Book*. "Everybody has the ability to learn, each in his own way."[4]

Whatever way they are characterized, students with learning differences face an uphill battle in the classroom. Sometimes they are not diagnosed for years. An educator may mistake a learning difference for laziness or stubbornness. Sometimes a teacher may even suspect a cognitive impairment. But learning differences are very different from cognitive impairment. The latter condition indicates a low potential for intellectual accomplishment. Cognitive impairment places a limit on what an individual will be able to accomplish. A learning difference poses no such restrictions. It simply requires a student to discover different learning strategies from the ones used in most classrooms.

Types of Learning Differences

The following are among the most common learning disabilities:

Dyslexia. Students with dyslexia have a hard time learning to read. For them, the printed page is like a code that they cannot decipher. It is estimated that eighty percent of all learning disabilities, or differences, involve reading. About 2 million children receive special help in school to deal with their reading problems.[5]

Dysgraphia. This learning difference makes it difficult for children to write legibly. They recognize words correctly, but they cannot copy them easily. When they are asked to write a sentence, their words may be jumbled together or take up too much space. Students with dysgraphia have a hard time staying between the lines. A teacher may mistakenly think such students are sloppy or do not care about their work.

Dyscalculia. Mathematics poses a great challenge to children with dyscalculia. They find it difficult to do calculations or understand math concepts like square roots or simple equations. Once again, this has nothing to do with a child's intelligence. What he or she needs is a different way to handle the material.

Auditory and Visual Processing Differences. Students dealing with these kinds of differences see and hear normally. However, they have problems understanding or interpreting what they see or hear. This, of course, makes learning in a traditional classroom setting difficult.

Attention Deficit Disorder (ADD)

Students with ADD do not have problems reading or doing math calculations. They are, however, easily distracted and may find it difficult to concentrate for prolonged periods. Instead of focusing on a single task, they are sensitive to their entire environment. Often they are impulsive, restless, and find it difficult to sit still. Let's imagine a child named Johnny. The rest of the class may be reading out loud, but Johnny runs to the window to observe a squirrel running up a tree. Then he wanders to the back of the room to examine the books, puzzles, and drawings on the bulletin board. He is interested in almost everything, but he cannot sit still. Forced to sit at his desk, Johnny becomes fidgety and jumpy. When a child's activity level becomes excessive in this way, psychologists say that he is hyperactive, and he is said to have attention deficit hyperactivity disorder (ADHD).

Sometimes it is a child's own thoughts that distract him or her. Take the imaginary example of Sandy. The teacher's blue sweater reminds her of the sky, which reminds her of clouds, which reminds her of flying through the clouds in an airplane. This then reminds her of visiting her Aunt Sonja in Florida, which reminds her of seeing crocodiles in the Everglades, and so on. Following her thoughts like a meandering stream,

Alexander Graham Bell received disappointing grades in school but was a gifted inventor. Some people have speculated that Bell had a learning disability.

Sandy comes to some very interesting places. She is a bright and imaginative child. But she completely misses the teacher's explanation of decimals.

Dealing with Learning Differences

Unfortunately, many schools have some difficulty dealing with the specific needs of students with learning differences. Teachers lack the time to give them individualized instruction. Yet these students with learning differences are expected to master the same material and complete the same assignments as everyone else. They have to meet the same requirements for promotion into the next grade or for graduation from high school. Although the situation sounds discouraging, schools are required by law to work out special accommodations that take a student's unique learning styles into consideration.

First, in order to qualify, the student has to be officially diagnosed by an educational specialist. This may involve answering questions and completing tests designed to reveal a student's strengths and weaknesses. Once the diagnosis is made, parents, teachers, and perhaps an educational psychologist develop a plan. This is called an individualized education plan, or IEP. Specific differences are taken into consideration and strategies worked out to help the child succeed. For example, children with learning differences often tire more quickly than their classmates. This leaves them with less energy to do their homework. What the teacher meant as a short assignment might take them hours. Under these circumstances, special accommodations might be made for homework. Perhaps the child has shorter assignments or is given time to work at school. Other accommodations might include more time to complete tests, special periods with a tutor, frequent

> Unfortunately, many schools have some difficulty dealing with the specific needs of students with learning differences.

The Porter Academy

Claudia Porter, founder of The Porter Academy in Roswell, Georgia, agrees that it is vital for all children to develop self-esteem. But the students who attend her private grade school have suffered a great deal of disappointment and frustration in school. "You need to work with the whole child to make her feel good about herself," Porter emphasizes.[6] Believing that a "pressure free" environment allows children to grow and learn most easily, Porter does not give grades. But teachers do assign homework. Exercise, occupational therapy, art, music, and drama are integrated into a curriculum that also focuses on the basics of reading, writing, and arithmetic. "I don't take behavior problems," explains Porter, "but I do take frustrated kids who are striking out because they don't know what else to do."[7] Porter and her staff teach them how to meet and master their unique challenges.

access to a computer, help with organization, or even someone to read test questions with them. It all depends on the individual student's strengths and weaknesses.

Collaborative Teaching

Sometimes a student's IEP may call for a collaborative teaching situation. This means two teachers collaborate or work together in the same class. One teaches the regular subject matter while the other provides support for students with learning differences. Special education teacher Joanna Hersch works with a science teacher at James River High School in Virginia. While the primary teacher presents the subject matter to the class, Hersch works with students on an individual basis. "I observe. I intervene," explained Hersch. "I make sure everything is understood. Some kids can't handle whatever stress is going on. The collaborative person helps." Students used to receiving poor grades may see their grades rise dramatically in a collaborative classroom. Hersch recalled a boy who started the class expecting to fail, worked hard, and was delighted to receive a C.

Not only did he acquire necessary study skills, he also made a giant leap in confidence.[8]

Teaching Students to Learn

Even students whose learning styles fit well with school routines can benefit from knowing more about how their minds work. Mel Levine believes that schools should teach children how their brains develop and learn.[9] Students can be taught techniques to help them pay attention, to memorize better, and to manage their time. Understanding the mind can also help kids develop social skills and enhance their creativity. According to Levine, everyone "should have an educational plan, one that sets goals and customizes learning."[10] In other words, all students should be treated as individuals. Schools exist for children, not children for schools.

Students with learning differences can become highly successful as they come to understand more about the way their minds and brains function. A boy who found school difficult once told Levine, "Sometimes I used to think I had real bad problems and I couldn't do anything about them. Then other times I thought I had no problem and was just plain lazy. Now I know I have a problem, a real problem that's not my fault and it's not so bad."[11]

Sometimes doctors prescribe medicines for students with trouble concentrating. Other children may learn to do well without taking any medication. Either way, a learning difference does not make it impossible to do well in school. The key to success is hard work, determination, and caring adults to help put students on the right path.

Some students thrive on lots of homework and tests. Jonas Salk, who developed a vaccine against polio in the 1950s, is an example of a student who did well under pressure. Salk's mother demanded top grades from her son, and he got them. At home he was encouraged to read as long as his books had no illustrations. Mrs. Salk considered books with pictures too frivolous for a serious student like her son. Jonas Salk became a model student. He was well-organized, studied hard, and helped classmates with difficult material.[1] A tough curriculum and careful supervision did not seem to bother Salk at all.

Albert Einstein, born in Germany in 1879, was a different

kind of student. He attended a very strict grade school and high school. Children had to sit quietly for hours. They were not supposed to ask questions about what they learned. Einstein hated to memorize facts. He thought school was boring and did not bother to hide his feelings. Despite Einstein's generally good grades, his teachers were angered and annoyed. One even told him that he would never amount to anything.[2] Finally, his teachers became so tired of Einstein's moodiness and disrespect- ful manners that they expelled him from high school. Yet today we remember Einstein as one of the smartest scientists who ever lived.

The stories of Jonas Salk and Albert Einstein reveal a broad spectrum in the ways children respond to school. They may be industrious and conscientious like Salk, rebellious and stubborn like Einstein, or anywhere in between. As we have seen, there is an equally wide range in the way students are able to handle academic pressure. Some students are naturally competitive; others are not. Some worry about living up to parental expecta- tions, while others may have fewer demands placed upon them by their families. Facing a rigorous curriculum, some students are overwhelmed easily; others take numerous tests and assign- ments in stride. Pressure does affect everyone at some time or other. There are ways to deal with it.

Review

To keep on top of your work and minimize stress, it helps to do a quick review of what goes on in your classes each day. By reviewing your history or science notes—even when it is not assigned—you allow the material to sink more deeply into your mind. You can think of this as the mental equivalent of highlighting text on a page. Regular reviews will help you learn material more quickly and efficiently.

That is what we're going to do in this final chapter: review. Some of the dos and don'ts listed below have already been mentioned in this book, but they're important enough to go over one more time. They can help you do well in school and beat stress at the same time.

Take care of yourself first. Eat wisely, and get enough sleep. Physical stress can make everything seem worse. You do not want to take a test tired or hungry.

Keep moving. A sign advertising a fitness club announces, "Stressed is desserts spelled backwards. Work off both." This is excellent advice. Psychologists say that exercise is one of the greatest of all stress-busters.

Carve your own space. This can be a room or part of one, a corner of the porch, a desk or table with a comfortable chair. This is your stress-free zone where you can relax, listen to music, read for pleasure, or simply think.

Be imaginative. It is not always easy to be creative when extracurricular activities engage you after school or when homework mounts. It pays to carve out a little time, maybe ten or fifteen minutes, for something you enjoy. It might be sketching, playing an instrument, cooking—whatever you find relaxing and fun.

Ask for help. If you're feeling worried because you do not understand a class or fear that you cannot keep up with the workload, tell someone. Parents, teachers, and counselors want what is best for you emotionally

> There is a wide range in the way students are able to handle academic pressure. Some students are overwhelmed easily; others take numerous tests and assignments in stride.

as well as academically. They may suggest tutoring or changing the level of your class. They may have study tips to offer. And they can reassure you that you're not alone in your academic challenges.

Keep track of your assignments. A little organization goes a long way. Maintain a regular study schedule. Write down when

As long as you focus on the assignments at hand, studying with friends can be very helpful.

assignments are due and plan how much time you need to complete them. Prioritize what needs to be done. Do not wait until the last minute to study for a test or begin a project.

Don't forget your friends are in the same boat. Studying with friends can be very helpful as long as you focus on the material to be covered. Quizzing each other is an excellent way to review for a test. A friend may be able to help you understand an algebra problem or a theory you did not quite grasp in history. When it is your turn to explain to someone else, you'll be reinforcing your own knowledge, too. And if you cannot get together in person, counselor Gail Hamilton recommends that friends coach each other over the phone.[3]

Don't fill up every waking moment. No one can do everything. Limit your after-school involvements. Do not feel you have to take part in everything to look good on your college application. Leadership teacher Sarah Mansfield advises students to be passionate about what they do. "Find your passion. Give 110% to what you love." It might be scouting or church activities or music or athletics. But, she cautions, "Don't sign up for everything."[4]

Don't make grades too important. Of course, you want to work for good grades. However, your whole future does not depend on your grades, your test scores, or where you go to college. Determination and enthusiasm count for more.

Don't compare yourself to others. Aim to do the best work you can do—not to beat your classmates. What you learn is more important than where you rank in the class.

Do something nice for someone. It does not have to big or time-consuming. You might stop to chat with an elderly neighbor, read a picture book to a younger sibling, or reach out to a classmate who seems lonely. Simple, quiet gestures can make a big difference to others. They also let you feel good about yourself. That is a huge stress-buster.

School should be more than hard work. Assistant principal Jennifer Coleman is adamant. "It should be about more than a grade. Learning is invigorating and great!"[5] Pleasure in new ideas and growing self-confidence should go hand-in-hand with learning. Sometimes a bit of academic pressure can be stimulating. Sometimes it feels overwhelming. The important thing to remember is that you can control the pressure. It does not have to control you.

Chapter Notes

Chapter 1 Kids on the Fast Track

1. Helen Wright, *Sweeper in the Sky: The Life of Maria Mitchell, First Woman Astronomer in America* (New York: The Macmillan Company, 1949).

2. Peg Tyre, "The New First Grade: Too Much Too Soon?" *Newsweek*, September 11, 2006, <http://www.msnbc.msn.com/id/14368573/site/newsweek/> (November 4, 2006).

3. Ibid.

4. Personal telephone interview with Marshall W. Trammell, Jr., December 10, 2008.

5. Alexandra Robbins, *The Overachievers: The Secret Lives of Driven Kids* (New York: Hyperion, 2006), p. 66.

6. David Elkind, *The Hurried Child: Growing Up Too Fast Too Soon* (Reading, Massachusetts: Addison-Wesley Publishing Company, 1981), p. 48.

7. Ibid.

8. William Crain, *Reclaiming Childhood: Letting Children Be Children in Our Achievement-Oriented Society* (New York: Henry Holt and Company, 2003), p. 150.

9. Ibid., p. 151.

Chapter 2 School Daze?

1. Personal telephone interview with Kim Sanford, October 7, 2007.

2. Ibid.

3. Alexandra Robbins, *The Overachievers: The Secret Lives of Driven Kids* (New York: Hyperion, 2006), p. 165.

4. Peg Tyre and Karen Springen, "Fourth-Grade Slump," *Newsweek*, February 19, 2007, p. 47.

5. Michael Thompson with Teresa Barker, *The Pressured Child: Freeing Our Kids from Performance Overdrive and Helping Them Find*

Success In School and Life (New York: Ballantine Books, 2005), p. 106.

6. Personal interview with students, October 25, 2007.

7. "Moving Up to Middle School," excerpted from "Moving to the Middle," published in the National PTA's *Our Children*, n.d., <http://www.school.familyeducation.com/parents-and-teacher/puberty/37581.html> (October 18, 2007).

8. Personal interview with Maryanne Kiley, October 25, 2007.

9. William Crain, *Reclaiming Childhood: Letting Children Be Children in Our Achievement-Oriented Society* (New York: Henry Holt and Company, 2003, p. 142.

10. Personal interview with Cynthia Ford, October 25, 2007.

11. Personal interview with Maryanne Kiley, October 25, 2007.

12. Personal interview with Colleen Twomey, October 25, 2007.

13. Personal interview with Dorene Jorgensen, October 25, 2007.

14. Personal interview with Bryan Carr, October 10, 2007.

15. Personal interview with Gail Hamilton, October 10, 2007.

16. Ibid.

17. Ibid.

18. Personal interview with Jennifer Coleman, October 10, 2007.

19. Personal interview with Sarah Mansfield, October 10, 2007.

20. Denise Clark Pope, *"Doing School": How We Are Creating a Generation of Stressed Out, Materialistic, and Miseducated Students* (New Haven, Conn.: Yale University Press, 2001), p. 156.

21. Personal interview with Jennifer Coleman, October 10, 2007.

Chapter 3 More Sources of Stress

1. WIST, "Quotations by Charles Schultz (1922–2000), American Cartoonist," *Peanuts*, 1963, <http://www.wist.info/s/schultz_charles/> (August 11, 2007).

2. Personal interview with Bryan Carr, October 10, 2007.

3. Susan Ohanian, *What Happened to Recess and Why Are Our*

Children Struggling in Kindergarten? (New York: McGraw-Hill, 2002), p. 57.

4. Alexandra Robbins, *The Overachievers: The Secret Lives of Driven Kids* (New York: Hyperion, 2006), p. 349.

5. Ibid., p. 350.

6. John Cloud, "Busy Is O.K. For Kids," *Time*, January 29, 2007, p. 51.

7. Christine Gross-Loh, "Give Me That Old-Time Recess," *Mothering*, March-April 2007, no. 141, p. 56.

8. Ibid.; and Ohanian, p. 2.

9. Gross-Loh, p. 56.

10. Ibid.

11. Robbins, p. 186.

12. Personal interview with Paul Fleisher, April 4, 2007.

13. Michael Thompson with Teresa Barker, *The Pressured Child: Freeing Our Kids from Performance Overdrive and Helping Them Find Success in School and Life* (New York: Ballantine Books, 2005), p. 195.

14. Robbins, p. 50.

15. Personal interview with Joanne Ward, October 7, 2007.

16. Personal telephone interview with Gail Hamilton, October 10, 2007.

Chapter 4 The Changing Face of Homework

1. Susan Ohanian, *What Happened to Recess and Why Are Our Children Struggling in Kindergarten?* (New York: McGraw-Hill, 2002), p. 207.

2. Ibid.

3. "Homework hours tripled since 1980," *CNN.com*, July 25, 2001, <http://www.archives.cnn.com/2001/fyi/teachers.ednews/07/25/homework.increase.ap/> (July 2, 2008).

4. Valerie Strauss, "Life Support: A history of homework," *Pittsburgh*

Post-Gazette.com, November 6, 2003, <http://www.post-gazette.com/lifestyle/20031106life6.asp> (November 5, 2006).

5. Marian Wilde, "How Much Homework Is Too Much?" *GreatSchools.net*, June 2006, <http://www.greatschools.net/cgi-bin/showarticle/ca/586> (July 17, 2008).

6. "History of Homework," *SFGate.com*, December 19, 1999, <http://www.sfgate.com/cgi-bin/article.cgi?file=examiner/archive/1999/12/19/NEWS4357.dtl> (November 6, 2006).

7. Brian P. Gill and Steven L. Schlossman, "Villain or Savior? The American Discourse on Homework, 1850–2003," *Theory Into Practice*, vol. 43, no. 3, 2004, College of Education, The Ohio State University, p. 175.

8. Ibid., p. 176.

9. "History of Homework."

10. Archived Information, *A Nation at Risk*, April 1983, <http://www.ed.gov/pubs/NatAtRisk/risk.html> (August 22, 2007).

11. Alfie Kohn, *The Homework Myth: Why Our Kids Get Too Much of a Bad Thing* (Cambridge, Mass.: Da Capo Press, 2006), p. 120.

12. Ibid.

Chapter 5 When Homework Gets You Down

1. Marian Wilde, "How Much Homework Is Too Much?" *GreatSchools.net*, June 2006, <http://www.greatschools.net/cgi-bin/showarticle/CA/586> (July 17, 2008).

2. Sara Bennett and Nancy Kalish, *The Case Against Homework: How Homework Is Hurting Our Children and What We Can Do About It* (New York: Crown Publishers, 2006), pp. 95–96.

3. Personal interview with Jeffrey Doyle, October 19, 2007.

4. "Rep. Lofgren Introduces ZZZ's to A's Act: Legislation Would Encourage Secondary Schools to Open Later," Press Release, October 19, 2007, <http://lofgren.house.gov/PRArticle.aspx?NewsID=1835> (October 20, 2007).

5. "Facts at Your Fingertips: Talking Points," National Sleep Foundation, n.d., <http://www.sleepfoundation.org/site/

c.hulXKjMOIxF/b.2511963/k.1926/Facts_at_Your_Fingertips> (October 20, 2007).

6. Ibid.

7. Alexandra Robbins, *The Overachievers: The Secret Lives of Driven Kids* (New York: Hyperion, 2006), p. 180.

8. Sara Bennett and Nancy Kalish, *The Case Against Homework: How Homework Is Hurting Our Children and What We Can Do About It* (New York: Crown Publishers, 2006), p. 259; David P. Baker and Gerald K. Le Tendre, *National Differences, Global Similarities: World Culture and the Future of Schooling* (Palo Alto, Calif. Stanford University Press, 2005).

9. Alfie Kohn, *The Schools Our Children Deserve: Moving Beyond Traditional Classroom and "Tougher Standards"* (Boston: Houghton Mifflin Company, 1999), p. 28.

10. Personal interview with Paul Fleisher, April 4, 2007.

11. Denise Clark Pope, *"Doing School": How We Are Creating a Generation of Stressed Out, Materialistic, and Miseducated Students* (New Haven, Conn.: Yale University Press, 2001), p. 60.

12. Personal interview with student, September 3, 2007.

Chapter 6 When the Government Gets Involved

1. Linda Perlstein, *Tested: One American School Struggles to Make the Grade* (New York: Henry Holt and Company, 2007), p. 235.

2. Ibid., p. 29.

3. Ibid.

4. *Tough Choices for Tough Times: The Report of the New Commission on the Skills of the American Workforce* (San Francisco: Jossey-Bass, 2007), p. xvi.

5. Ibid.

6. Ibid., p. xix.

7. Neal P. McCluskey, *Feds in the Classroom: How Big Government Corrupts, Cripples, and Compromises American Education* (New York: Rowman & Littlefield Publishers, 2007), p. 60.

8. Ibid.

9. Ibid., p. 64.

10. Ibid.; and "The Truth about National Testing," *Phyllis Schlafly Report*, November 1997.

11. Perlstein, p. 32.

12. Greg Toppo, "How Bush education law has changed our schools," *USATODAY.com*, January 7, 2007, <http://www.usatoday.com/news/education/2007-01-07-no-child_x.htm> (September 3, 2007).

13. "Statement by U.S. Secretary of Education Margaret Spellings on the No Child Left Behind Act of 2007," Press Release, July 12, 2007, <http://www.edgov/news/pressreleases/2007/07/07122007a.html> (September 3, 2007).

14. Perlstein, p. 120.

15. Ibid., p. 123.

16. Personal interview with Joanne Ward, May 2007.

17. Personal interview with Paul Fleisher, April 4, 2007.

18. Personal interview with Mickey VanDerwerker, July 25, 2007.

19. Personal interview with Marion Sammartino, July 24, 2007.

20. Personal interview with Mickey VanDerwerker, July 25, 2007.

21. Ibid.

22. "Parents Across Virginia United to Reform SOLs," n.d., <http://www.solreform.org/> (July 14, 2008).

23. Perlstein, p. 201.

24. Ibid.

25. David Elkind, *The Hurried Child: Growing Up Too Fast Too Soon* (Reading, Massachusetts: Addison-Wesley Publishing Company, 1981), p. 55.

26. Wayne Jennings, "School Transformation," 2004, <http://www.waynejennings.net/brain_pages/20040722173147.html> (July 14, 2008).

27. Lisa Chipongian, "Where Did the '12 Brain-Mind Learning Principles' Come From?" Brain Connection, n.d.,

<http://www.brainconnection.com/topics/?main=fa/
brain-based3#A1> (July 14, 2008).

Chapter 7 The College Game

1. Mel Levine, *A Mind at a Time* (New York: Simon & Schuster, 2002), pp. 335–336.

2. Ibid., p. 332.

3. Alexandra Robbins, *The Overachievers: The Secret Lives of Driven Kids* (New York: Hyperion, 2006), p. 134.

4. Ibid.; and personal interview with Jennifer Coleman, October 19, 2007.

5. "Student sues to get A+, not A," *CNN.com*, February 6, 2003, <http://www.cnn.com/2003/EDUCATION/02/06/a.plus.ap/index.html> (May 12, 2008).

6. Robbins, p. 134.

7. Ibid., p. 300.

8. Richard Rudin, "Testing Your Patience," *How To Get Into College 2008*, Newsweek/Kaplan, p. 28.

9. Ibid., p. 29.

10. Alec Klein, *A Class Apart: Prodigies, Pressure, and Passion Inside of One of America's Best High Schools* (New York: Simon & Schuster, 2007), p. 31.

11. Ibid.

12. Personal interview with Bryan Carr, October 10, 2007.

13. Jonathan Alter, "Stop the Madness," *How to Get Into College 2008*, Newsweek/Kaplan, p. 10.

14. Personal interview with Bryan Carr, October 19, 2007.

15. Richard Johnson, "Look Who Harvard Blew Off," *New York Post*, May 22, 2007, <http://www.nypost.com/seven/05222007/gossip/pagesix/look_who_harvard_blew_off_pagesix_html> (September 15, 2007).

16. Personal interview with Mickey VanDerwerker, July 25, 2005.

Chapter 8 Negative Fallout from Stress

1. Mel Levine, *A Mind at a Time* (New York: Simon & Schuster, 2002), p. 264.

2. Ibid.

3. Personal interview with Autumn Nabors, October 10, 2007.

4. Bettie B. Youngs, *Stress and Your Child: Helping Kids Cope with the Strains and Pressures of Life* (New York: Ballantine Books, 1985), p. 151.

5. Alexandra Robbins, *The Overachievers: The Secret Lives of Driven Kids* (New York: Hyperion, 2006), p. 96.

6. Alfie Kohn, *The Schools Our Children Deserve: Moving Beyond Traditional Classrooms and "Tougher Standards"* (Boston: Houghton Mifflin Company, 1999), p. 30.

7. Susan Ohanian, *What Happened to Recess and Why Are Our Children Struggling in Kindergarten?* (New York: McGraw-Hill, 2002), p. 79.

8. Kathy Slobogin, "Survey: Many students say cheating's OK," *CNN.com/Education*, April 5, 2002, <http://www.archives.cnn.com/2002/fyi/teachers.ednews/05/05/highschool...> (November 3, 2006).

9. Robbins, p. 97.

10. Denise Clark Pope, *"Doing School": How We Are Creating a Generation of Stressed Out, Materialistic, and Miseducated Students* (New Haven, Conn.: Yale University Press, 2001), p. 40.

11. Ibid.

12. "Statistics: Eating Disorders and their Precursors," National Eating Disorders Association, <http://www.sc.edu/healthycarolina/pdf/facstaffstu/eatingdisorders/EatingDisorderStatistics.pdf> (September 27, 2007).

13. "Anorexia Nervosa—Topic Overview," WebMD, n.d., <http://www.webmd.com/mental-health/anorexia-nervosa/anorexia-nervosa-topic-overview > (September 27, 2007).

14. "Bulimia Nervosa—Topic Overview," WebMD, n.d., <http://www.

webmd.com/mental-health/bulimia-nervosa/bulimia-nervosa-topic-overview> (September 27, 2007).

15. "Binge Eating Disorder," Athealth.com., January 2, 2008, <http://www.athealth.com/Consumer/disorders/Bingeeating.html> (September 27, 2007).

16. Personal interview with Sarah Mansfield, October 10, 2007.

Chapter 9 Different Learning Styles

1. Patricia Polacco, *Thank You, Mr. Falker* (New York: Philomel Books, 1998).

2. Charlotte Gray, *Reluctant Genius: Alexander Graham Bell and the Passion for Invention* (New York: Arcade Publishing, 2006), p. 11.

3. Ibid., p. 204.

4. Nancy S. Boyles, M.Ed. and Darlene Contadino, M.S.W., *The Learning Differences Sourcebook* (Los Angeles: Lowell House, 1997), pp. 16–17.

5. Sally Shaywitz, *Overcoming Dyslexia: A New and Complete Science-Based Program for Reading Problems at Any Level* (New York: Alfred A. Knopf, 2003), p. 29.

6. Personal telephone interview with Claudia Porter, October 9, 2007.

7. Ibid.

8. Personal interview with Joanna Hersch, October 10, 2007.

9. Mel Levine, *A Mind at a Time* (New York: Simon & Schuster, 2002), pp. 315–319.

10. Ibid., p. 322.

11. Ibid., p. 278.

Chapter 10 Stress-Busters

1. Richard Carter, *Breakthrough: The Saga of Jonas Salk* (New York: Trident, 1966).

2. Ronald W. Clark, *Einstein: The Life and Times*, 2nd edition (New York: Avon Books, 1984).

3. Personal telephone interview with Gail Hamilton, October 10, 2007.

4. Personal interview with Sarah Mansfield, October 10, 2007.

5. Personal interview with Jennifer Coleman, October 10, 2007.

Glossary

adequate yearly progress (AYP)—A way to evaluate a school's effectiveness based on the annual improvement in students' standardized test scores. A minimum AYP is required by the No Child Left Behind Act.

anorexia—An eating disorder, primarily afflicting young women, in which a person eats so little that she becomes emaciated.

attention deficit disorder (ADD)—A learning disability or difference that is characterized by impulsivity and distractibility.

auditory processing difference—A learning disability, or difference, that affects the way students learn spoken material.

benchmarks—Standards that students are required to meet on state-mandated tests.

binge eating—Compulsive overeating.

block scheduling—A school schedule that features fewer class periods but allows students to study each subject more intensely.

bulimia—An eating disorder, primarily affecting young women, in which a person eats large amounts of food, and then purges herself.

cognitive impairment—A condition that limits what an individual may learn or accomplish.

collaborative teaching—A situation in which one teacher covers the subject matter while another teacher provides support for students with learning disabilities.

cybercheating—A very risky practice of buying papers over the Internet.

depression—A psychiatric condition that may be characterized by feelings of sadness, lack of energy, and an inability to concentrate as well as other symptoms.

dyscalculia—A learning disability, or difference, that affects the way a student learns mathematics.

dysgraphia—A learning disability, or difference, that affects a student's handwriting.

dyslexia—A learning disability, or difference, that affects the way a student learns to read.

early decision—An option in which applicants to a particular college may be accepted several months before the main body of students.

grade point average (GPA)—Overall average of all the grades a student has taken in which an A counts for 4 points, B for 3, C for 2, D for 1. In AP classes an extra point is added.

individualized education plan (IEP)—A set of special accommodations tailored to meet the specific needs of students with learning disabilities, or differences.

learning disability—One of several conditions in which a student's brain may process information differently from the way the majority of his or her classmates do. Children with learning disabilities, or differences, may require special techniques to master educational skills.

No Child Left Behind Act—Federal legislation that mandates standardized tests at designated grades and imposes penalties on schools with low test scores.

overachiever—Term used to designate a student who succeeds beyond the expectations of his or her teachers and counselors.

pacing charts—Schedules that dictate the rate at which teachers must present specific matter.

Preliminary Scholastic Aptitude Test (PSAT)—A test taken by college-bound students in preparation for the Scholastic Aptitude Test (SAT).

progressive movement—An educational philosophy, popular in the 1930s, that looked beyond academics to focus on the physical and emotional needs of students.

SAT Reasoning Test (formerly known as the Scholastic Aptitude Test or the Scholastic Achievement Test)—A test taken by college-bound students to gauge their potential for verbal and mathematical learning.

SAT Subject Tests (formerly known as achievement tests or SAT IIs)—College entrance exams that test a student's aptitude in a particular subject like geometry or French.

Standards of Learning Tests (SOLs)—State-mandated standardized tests administered in Virginia.

student burnout—A condition whereby students lose motivation and interest in their studies.

test anxiety—A condition in which students become overly fearful of taking tests.

underachiever—Term used to designate a student who does not measure up to what teachers consider to be his or her potential.

visual processing difference—A learning disability, or difference, that affects the way a student perceives written material.

Further Reading

Erlbach, Arlene. *The Middle School Survival Guide.* New York: Walker & Co, 2003.

Esherick, Joan. *Balancing Act: A Teen's Guide to Managing Stress.* Philadelphia: Mason Crest Publishers, 2005.

Fox, Annie, and Ruth Kirschner. *Too Stressed to Think? A Teen Guide to Staying Sane When Life Makes You Crazy.* Minneapolis: Free Spirit Publishing, 2005.

Fox, Janet S. *Get Organized Without Losing It.* Minneapolis: Free Spirit Publishing, 2006.

Hyde, Margaret O., and Elizabeth H. Forsyth. *Stress 101: An Overview for Teens.* Minneapolis: Twenty-first Century Books, 2008.

Muster, Regina. *College Knowledge: The A+ Guide to Early College Planning.* Eagleville, Pa.: DNA Press, 2004.

Toronto Public Library. *Research Ate My Brain: The Panic-Proof Guide to Surviving Homework.* Annick Press, 2005.

Internet Addresses

"Coping With School Stress"
   **<http://www.webmd.com/parenting/features/
   coping-school-stress>**

"High School: It's Academic"
   **<http://pbskids.org/itsmylife/school/highschool/
   article5.html>**

"Homework Help"
   **<http://kidshealth.org/kid/grow/school_stuff/
   homework_help.html>**

Index